Initial

Deception

Prequel to *Nebulous Deception*

The Connie Womack
Series

By Brent Hensley

[handwritten inscription: To my new friend — Nancy — Brent Hensley 9-8-22]

Dedication

I dedicate this book to a

wonderful man, my uncle,

Wm. Keith Faulkner,

who stepped into the shoes of father

after the passing of my dad.

We love you always,

Uncle Billy.

Initial Deception

List of Characters

Insurance Investigator—Connie Sue Womack

Connie's Husband—Jack Randall Womack

Jack's Right-Hand Man—Rhys Garret

Connie's Best Friend—Dr. Kay Shirley

Connie's Boss—Bob Wesson

Bob Wesson's Wife—Nancy

Adversary—Cecil "Chief" Locklear

Cecil's Cohort—Thomas "Skeeter" Wise

Jack's Special Forces Team—

    Steve Hyatt, aka "Hotel"

    Ray Putnam, aka "Rain Man"

    Phil Owens, aka "Oil Can"

    Randall Remick, aka "Recoil"

New York City Detective—Chris Tighe

Washington, DC, Head Detective—Matt Baranski

Washington, DC, Detective—Tommy Riddle

Computer Technician—Daniel Gambaro

Daniel Gambaro's Wife—Kimberly

Jack's Old Friend and Mentor—Sam Hornaday

Lloyd's of London Manager—Linwood Massey

Tel-Net Employee—Ronnie Sawyer

Jack's Security Men—Ray Ketchum and

Sydney "Spider" Rountree

Jack's Friend—Lieutenant Commander

Harry Wagner

Ambassador's Assistant—Candace Martin

And Tricks the Cat

Prologue

Connie loves her new life in the Charleston area, as she looks out across Shem Creek from the house she rents in Mt. Pleasant. The sun is on its steady retreat, dropping just below the horizon, offering serenity as well as nature's beauty. She slowly sips on a glass of red wine, leaving her with a slight smile on her lips. Looking out towards Charleston Harbor she watches the slow parade of fishing boats majestically gliding up and down the waterway as if the calendar has been turned back to the 1800s.

The landscape is as enchanting as an oil painting from the great impressionist Monet, with the brilliant colors of orange, fuchsia, and gold spilling onto the natural canvas of the low-country sky. It pleases Connie as she sits in her wheelchair taking in the tranquil sights of the tall sea grass, slow-moving waters, and beautiful wildlife dotting the landscape. Her thoughts as to why she moved down here to Charleston are not as serene as the landscape.

No, her departure from DC was quick and abrupt. It was not in the manner she would have chosen if she had felt she had a choice. After all, who could just sit back and not try to help when kidnapped children are involved? But things have a way of working out.

Even the professional relationship between Connie and the Charleston Police Chief, Tommy John Parnell, seems to be more relaxed as they began to see things more eye to eye. It all started when the mayor of Charleston insisted that Chief Parnell call for her help in Washington, DC, requesting her services, and that was the main cause that got her to come down here in the first place.

No, this low country of South Carolina suits Connie Womack just fine as she feels the warm evening breeze sweep across the porch. How she got here really doesn't matter to her at this point, and regardless of how, the change is welcome after dealing with all the uncertainty for the last few years, and now without Jack in her life. But she still misses him terribly and wonders why her loss of him still seems so hard to bear.

After all, as she thinks back to when they started their new marriage, being separated from Jack is not a new challenge for her. They often were separated for months at a time. As an insurance investigator, Connie would often be off in some country trying to find stolen artifacts, and Jack, a Navy commander, was always off trying to save the world, one military campaign at a time.

The smell of the fresh ocean breezes once again causes her to daydream, the fresh ocean breezes of Charleston taking her back to the salty bay breezes of Annapolis, Maryland, when she was a lot younger. The sights and smells of the sea air cause her thoughts to come rushing back to when they first got married and were living in a small house on the water outside

Annapolis. She had a new life and marriage with the love of her life and hopes that someday they would settle down and have a child or two and maybe live a so-called normal life, but that would never happen. And as the years went by, that too was OK to Connie as long as she had her Jack.

She is an insurance investigator now, retired after 20 years from the Army's Military Police, travelling all around the world. No longer will she sit in that old rocking chair looking out over the Chesapeake Bay just waiting for Jack. Being ex-military, Connie considers herself a very independent woman, but she also loved her life as a wife. She never minded waiting for her Jack to come home. After all those campaigns, despite if he was on a small mission or in a full-scale war, Connie was always there welcoming him back home. But the thought of him never returning is still unbearable as she thinks back to his last mission: the one mission that would forever change both their lives and the one memory she could never forget. Nor would she ever forget the people who were responsible for making it so . . .

Last

Mission

Iraq

Chapter 1

THE ARABIAN NIGHT SKY ROARED TO
LIFE as operation "Shock and Awe" commenced with
an overwhelming spectacular display of force as
thousands of antitank, ground-to-air ballistic missiles,
Scud rockets, and military ordinances of all varieties
found their target. These ordinances were from the
militaries of over 35 different nations and were
unleashed upon the once calm and peaceful desert of
Iraq in response to Iraq's invasion and annexation of
Kuwait on August 2, 1990.

The sheer force of the explosions awoke not only
the sleepy landscape of sand dunes and camels, but the
entire world in this coalition's show of world defiance, as
the unleashing of these ammunitions quickly catapulted

this once thriving but still ancient civilization straight into the 20th century. This event occurred on January 17, 1991, as Operation Desert Storm was officially underway.

The sky was full as hundreds of aircraft of all types dotted the night sky. Aboard one of those planes was soon to be retired Commander Jackson Randall Womack of the elite Navy SEALs. Jack was heading up a handpicked team comprised of all the different branches from the US Special Forces. But he was reluctant to take on such a mission. It was not just because he was a short-timer but also because he preferred working with his own men. But the politicians in the White House wanted to show solidarity among the armed forces.

Short-timer or not, with his retirement being less than one month away, Jack had to admit he was the most qualified man to lead the group. After all, he had already spent months heading up the first of several undercover missions, which were located deep in the countries of Iraq and Kuwait. He and his men had already gathered hundreds of critical pieces of intelligence from behind enemy lines.

Jack's new assignment was to be dropped somewhere near the city of Bagdad under the cover of night, setting up strategic and vital communication lines for the US-led forces. That's what was on paper, but secretly his main objective was to take out Iraq's leader, Saddam Hussein—a regular day at the office for a man like Jackson Womack, one of the most decorated officers in the US Navy. There seemed to be no job too tough, or at least that's the way it had been his whole career. But this one felt different to Jack. This one would keep him up at night causing him to wonder with second thoughts about what didn't feel right about this mission. He could not put his finger on why this mission didn't feel right. His thoughts were abruptly interrupted as the pilot relayed information of the drop zone into Jack's headset.

"Sir, we are closing in on the drop zone and should be over the area in about 10 minutes." The news caused Jack to sit up straight in his seat as the reality of the moment came crashing in, and he knew it was game time, regardless of his uneasy intuition.

The mission came first as he called back to the pilot, "Roger that flight deck." Jack sat chewing on the end of an unlit cigar. He paused for a second taking a look down the line at his men who were still checking their gear. He watched as they rehearsed and studied their assigned tasks, all the while getting ready and making sure by checking and rechecking their equipment, which varied from night vision glasses and oxygen masks to their array of weapons and ammo. At the same time the men were bouncing up and down off their seats from the explosions of the antiaircraft fire which rocked and rattled the old C-130 Hercules aircraft.

Then in one swift motion the men could feel the pushing pressure of g-forces as the aircraft broke away from the formation of the other planes and began its steep corkscrew climb for more altitude and less visibility, rising up into the safety blanket of heavy cloud coverage. Jack paid special attention to the two newest members of his team as he noticed little signs of being nervous.

Cecil "Chief" Locklear and Thomas "Skeeter" Wise, the two Rangers, were the two newest members of the team of eight, and why not be a little nervous? After all it was their first real battle, Jack thought, as he watched their hands shake. All eight men including Jack were a little nervous; they would not be human if that wasn't the case. But he knew and trusted the other five men who had all fought side by side in several campaigns, the last being in Honduras in operation Golden Pheasant.

Once again now they were just a few pounds of the 140 thousand pounds of payload this huge aircraft was carrying. And for these Navy SEALs, Airborne Rangers, and Delta Force men it was going to be a quick one-way flight down to the desert sand dunes below. Jack's thoughts quickly turned to his beautiful wife Connie as he took his last look at her picture, and with a quick kiss he then tucked it back into his shirt pocket, as the jump lights flashed yellow a couple of times signaling the jump site was soon approaching.

"All right, gentlemen, it's zero hour, look sharp be sharp," Jack announced as he stood. The rest of the men repeated his action and took their position facing the back of the aircraft. Jack started the slow walk giving each of the seven men a quick inspection and either a pat on the shoulder or a pull on a strap or two, along with a firm handshake, and always a smile. Jack wanted to make sure each one knew Jack would be right behind them, and no matter what, he would do anything he could to make sure they made it back stateside alive.

"Stow away that blade Ranger Locklear, you don't want to accidentally land on that thing, do you?"

"No sir, I mean yes sir, Commander Womack," said one of the newest team members as he tried to replace the knife back into its sheaf correctly. Jack reached out and patted the young soldier on the shoulder, then straightened his parachute lanyard to make sure it was in its proper position. Down the line he did likewise to all the others. Jack also worked on his pep talk as he carried on his inspections with each man till he reached the end of the line, and of course standing there in front of them all was his best man and friend, Lieutenant Rhys Garret.

"Are we ready to go, Rhys?" Jack asked, as the whole team stood at attention and ready to jump.

"Sir, yes sir!" said Rhys, as the whole chorus of excited men repeated his statement as they shouted out in unison, "Yes sir," which made Jack smile with pride.

Suddenly lights started flashing and alarms sounded as the cargo bay went totally dark till the red jump lights began to blink as the back-payload door slowly opened. The men were quickly greeted by a big blast of Iraqi night air as it rushed in filling the compartment. A couple of minutes went by, the red jump light switched to yellow as the sound of the alarm shifted to more of a high-pitched tone beeping in their ears. Once the cargo door was securely locked in its downward position, the call was given.

"Let's get in position boys. It's about time to rock," shouted Rhys Garret. With that everyone started edging their way closer to the end of the ramp, all the while making last-minute adjustments with their gear. Rhys then signaled to everyone to turn on their oxygen supply on their helmets, with everyone knowing this happened right before their descent. The men stood side by side in groups of two as they waited. Slowly they seemed to inch up a little closer to the bold red line painted on the deck of the bay door as each man anticipated the word to be given. To the rookies the waiting seemed to last forever. Then like a shot of cold water of reality the alarm sounded with a steady blast as the flashing light turned bright green.

Everyone shouted, "Go! Go! Go!" Each group of two jumped face-first entering the dark night sky, falling into the unknown abyss that lay beneath. In tandem they all jumped as Jack counted out loud, and then it was his and Rhys's turn as they too stepped up to the red line, and with a thumbs up and a quick prayer they stepped off the platform into the black darkness of the Arabian night.

Jack heard the oxygen pour through his mask as he did his best Darth Vader impression with the excitement causing his heart rate to increase from the thrill of the jump taking over his senses. It never gets old, he thought, as he assessed the situation and located his men. Both he and Rhys folded their arms down closely to their bodies, quickly turning themselves into a rocket as they were pointing in the right direction with heads downward to catch up with the others. Jack felt the pressure of his G-suit as it filled up with more air now that he was flying at speeds well over 150 miles an hour. Still the only thing on his mind was the mission.

Despite political critics and news pundits, his men were there for one thing and one thing only. It was not to invade this nation below his feet, but to free a country and its people from a terrifying dictator and brutal tyrant named Saddam Hussein. And that was the only reason he and his men needed to know and to understand. As Jack and Rhys quickly approached their small band of liberators, Jack quickly applied the speed brakes, opening his arms and legs spread-eagle causing the air to catch him. Putting a stop to his missile-like descent he cozied right up to his team in an aerobatic freefall.

"Everyone good here," Jack called out as he caught his breath and did a quick head count.

"Yes sir, so far so good," answered Rhys Garret. The rest of the men started to laugh as they started to think of the old joke of the man that fell out of an airplane and passed a sky-diver. When asked if he was OK the man answered, "so far so good."

"OK men you all know your assignments. We'll break off from each other at an altitude of 13,000 feet and meet up at 03:00 hours at the TRK, (Tigris River Bridge in the Karada section of Baghdad). Everyone good with that?"

"Yes sir, roger that," shouted the circle of eight, as they fell like a rock, at a speed of 1,000 feet a minute, roughly 120 mph.

It didn't seem very long before they noticed the fast-approaching ground as the landscape was swiftly rising up to meet them. As their disbursement altitude was reached the group was on the ready to break apart as Commander Womack shouted "Now!" And at that point all eight pieces of the circle scattered in several different directions.

The New Recruits

Chapter 2

THE HOT SUMMER SUN BORE DOWN ON THE TWO young soldiers trying not to look too conspicuous wearing civilian clothing, but the way they carried themselves along with their haircuts still gave them away. They walked with a brisk pace crossing the busy street trying to escape the southern heat as they arrived at the Treasure Chest Gentlemen's Club. The club was actually a topless bar on Hay Street in the seedy red-light district of Fayetteville, North Carolina, and located only a few miles from their Ranger base at Fort Bragg.

They both stopped long enough to nervously look up and down the street to see if they were being followed before cautiously opening the door. The cool of the air-conditioning welcomed them as they stepped inside for sanctuary. They both stopped and removed their sunglasses, allowing their eyes to adjust to the dimly lit bar room which smelled like stale beer and dried sweat. The sound of disco music was playing in the background. The bright light from outside caused the bartender to notice the new customers standing in the doorway.

"Hey fellows, we're closed, don't open till six o'clock," shouted the bartender as he multitasked on bar prep, cleaning glasses, and watching a couple of girls on stage practicing their new routine. The two newcomers quickly noticed their host who fit the description they were given over the phone. It was no doubt that was the man who invited them. He was sitting in the corner of the room next to the stage, strangely wearing sunglasses and a bright green suit with large white stripes as instructed.

"He's not exactly keeping a low profile is he," said one to the other as they walked deeper into the bar and closer to the stage floor. "We're with him," pointed the tall one, as the bartender stopped cleaning and put down the glasses as if he was going to stop their entry.

"It's OK Danny, they're with me. Monsieurs, please over here," shouted and waved the odd-looking little man with a French accent. "Please have a seat, right here," as he patted the hard wooden chair with his hand as if it had a seat cushion. Still showing signs of nerves, the two men first looked around the dimly lit bar before taking their seats. Their attention was quickly diverted to the stage, watching the nightly entertainment without saying a word.

There were no other customers in the place, just chairs after chairs stacked on top of the tables. The soundtrack of Saturday Night Fever and the brothers Gibbs played loudly on the overhead speakers as two topless dancers, Darla and Rachel, took turns twisting and spinning like gymnasts on the pole on center stage.

"Do you like what you see, gentlemen?" The odd-looking man watched the two soldiers staring as if they were in a trance as they watched the two semi-nude dancers. He then turned to the bartender. "Danny, drinks for my friends. What would you like, gentlemen?" That broke the spell.

"I'll have a beer, Budweiser please," nervously said the smaller of the two men. The larger one looked down at his friend as if he needed permission. The stare quickly made him change his mind.

"That's OK, sir. I'm fine. I don't need anything," as he looked over at his buddy hoping to receive redemption. The larger man with dark skin began to talk. "You deal with me little man, I will do the talking."

"Yes monsieur, I understand you are in charge, oui. You must be the one they call Chief, a Native American I believe your kind likes to be called. And you are Thomas and I understand you like to be called Skeeter?"

"Cecil will be fine, Frenchie. You can call me Cecil."

The Frenchman never told them his real name and didn't seem to mind the word "Frenchie." "Fine,

Monsieur Cecil, I will." Turning towards the stage he yelled, "Girls that's enough please. Stop, you can leave us now, girls please. And Danny please have someone turn off that confounded music."

The two girls jumped a little as they suddenly realized they were not alone. Then without hesitation one girl hurriedly helped the other down from the pole as they rapidly picked up their things. The bartender-turned stagehand turned off the music as ordered. "Now that's better, we can hear ourselves talk. Now gentlemen first things first, before we get started you two must always remember you will be working for the organization, not me. I'm nothing but a spokesperson. They give the orders. I only make sure they are completed. And trust me gentlemen, once you do this task you will be a part of the organization and there will be no turning back, do you understand me?"

"Yeah, and if we say no now, then what, we end up dead and buried out in some swamp around here? No, we are committed wholeheartedly. We are dedicated to the cause monsieur," said Cecil, as Skeeter agreed by shaking his head yes.

"Very well then," Frenchie said as he pulled a manila envelope out of his coat pocket and laid it on the table in front of the two soldiers. Cecil reached out to retrieve it, but suddenly the man's hand quickly came down on top of Cecil's hand holding both his hand and the envelope. "Not so fast monsieur. The money will come soon enough, but first I need you to take care of some pressing but delicate business."

Cecil pulled his hand free as Frenchie pulled a piece of folded paper out of his coat and placed it on the table. Here is your assignment Monsieurs, but unfortunately this is not the TV show *Mission Impossible*. You do not have a choice whether you can accept your assignment or not. When you two agreed to work for the organization, your choice was made. Again, do you understand me? I am very serious."

"What do you want us to do Frenchie, kill someone?"

"No sir, nothing like that Monsieur Cecil, Monsieur Skeeter. You see it has come to our attention that one of the two dancers, you know the girls who were just on stage here, is working as an undercover agent, no pun intended," as he smiled. "She must be very good under the covers I'm sure, but they need to go," he laughed.

"Need to go where?" Skeeter asked, as Cecil turned and looked at his partner.

"Don't be so inpatient gentlemen. I just need you to escort them to my airplane this evening. It's located at a small airport outside of Lumberton about 40 miles south of here off the interstate."

"I know where it is," said Cecil.

"Is that when you are going to kill them?" asked Skeeter.

"No, Monsieurs, they will not be killed. The organization is not like that. No, they will be simply shipped off, I believe this time it's to India. They are to be a surprise gift for one who graciously sponsors the organization."

"Shipped, you mean like cattle," said Skeeter

"No, I mean like sex slaves."

Both men did not know what to say. This was all new to them. Chief looked down at the little man after hearing that news. "Back home if someone got out of line you just killed them and let the alligators eat 'em. But a life in sex-trafficking, being a human sex-slave, that sounds worse."

Skeeter looked surprised. "I thought we were here to discuss the Iraq mission, not some housekeeper problem you boys are having."

"Monsieur Skeeter please, you both are one of us now. So if the organization is having problems it too is your problem. As far as Iraq, you two will be receiving information on that mission in a few days but this matter needs to be handled first."

Chief looked over at Skeeter as to say shut up. Then he turned back toward Frenchie. "We understand, we got it, OK. Now about the girls, where do we find them?"

"It's all on this piece of paper. The girls live together out back in one of those apartments; the number is on the paper. I will meet you at the airport 11 o'clock tonight. And Monsieurs do not disappoint me, or

this will be a real short stint of time for you boys
working for the organization."

"Don't worry Frenchie, you can count on us. You
just be there at 11 o'clock. I hope you won't be late," said
Cecil as he and Skeeter stood up. Cecil looked back
down at the little man. "Merci pour l'hospitalite,"
showing Frenchie he could speak French as well.

Cecil was feeling pretty good about himself and
the whole situation as they walked back to the front
door of the bar. His partner, however, was having
second thoughts. Skeeter could not help but wonder
what he just got himself into. Quickly the two placed
their sunglasses back on their faces and braced
themselves for the summer heat and bright sunshine
before opening the bar door to the new world they had
just entered.

Diamonds & Doughnuts

Chapter 3

ON HER HANDS AND KNEES CONNIE PAINSTAKINGLY searched through literally thousands of pieces of broken glass with her tweezers as she placed the newfound evidence into the plastic bag. "That makes that one 147," she thought as she numbered the newest bag placing it in a big blue plastic tub along with all the others. Being too heavy to carry, she dragged the tub across the floor.

"Thanks a lot, guys," she said aloud as she looked over at couple of policemen shooting the bull while eating out of a now empty doughnut box. *They had done about all they could to contaminate the crime scene. Finding a clue, now that would truly be above their two pay grades.* She slowly stood straight up, rubbing her sore back and at the same time looking around the store making sure not to miss anything else that appeared to look broken, missing, or out of place. After all, this was the famous Tiffany's, the prestigious jewelry store. The curiosity of the whole thing had caused dozens of onlookers to peer all day through the windows of the 5th Avenue store in downtown Manhattan.

Once again she looked at the doughnut boys and shouted, "Hey, you two, will you please go outside to eat? We have a crime scene that's screwed up enough. I don't want to find pieces of doughnuts in with my evidence bags." The two in blue looked like two grazing cows chewing their cuds. Doughnuts were still hanging out of their mouths as they tried to talk. "Sorry lady, but like I said earlier, the department has already investigated this joint. The chief said this place is clear to walk in."

"Hey guys if you want to help please get out of here!" They were still watching her when she shouted, "Now already!"

"Now, now, Connie Womack, I know you're tired and a bit upset, and hey you have every right to be, but sweetheart, you can't talk like that to New York's finest," said Bob Wesson standing on the other side of the display counter.

"Bob, you startled me. I didn't see you come in." She started to brush off floor lint, trying to straighten up her appearance a bit. Bob Wesson was Connie's boss, a fair guy to work for; he looked to be in his late 50s or early 60s she guessed, average height, a little round in the belly and a little thin on the top, and gray on the sides. He had worked himself up to the top in the insurance business starting as sales agent, then an investigator like Connie, but he wasn't too good she was told, and now he was the owner of the company after the founder Samuel Hartwell died. They had been drinking buddies.

But Bob loved Connie, and if he was ever in the same area where she was working he tended to pop in, especially if TV cameras and reporters were present. After all, she was his number one investigator, and he had been one of her husband's friends for years. "Those goons don't know any better, sweetheart, it's OK!" He grabbed her hand and put one of the plastic bags of evidence on one of the only jewelry counters that wasn't broken.

"Bob, what are you doing here? Bob, don't walk over there, no Bob stop!" she shouted. "Mr. Wesson, can't you hear?" He knew then she was mad since she addressed him as Mr. Wesson. "You, too, are contaminating the crime scene. Don't touch anything please!" She took the bag he had just grabbed and placed it into the plastic tub as well.

"Well, how's it going?" he said, as he dusted off his hands.

"Fine, Bob, it's going just fine, but I can't do my job with you in here. You need to leave so I can solve this thing. OK, Bob?"

"Sure, sure Connie, but remember this is a big one. The owners are saying the thieves got away with, get this Connie, $1.9 million. Connie, that's the largest robbery in Tiffany's 157-year history. It's the biggest period, with over 400 necklaces, 100 rings, and no telling how many loose diamonds, and all large carats." He pulled out his handkerchief as little beads of sweat appeared on his forehead.

"You have to crack this case. My company can't afford this much. I will lose everything. Do you understand? There will be no more Hartwell and Wesson Insurance Company, gone, everything gone."

"Bob, once more," she shouted with hands on her hips this time as she glared at him. "Stop it and let me do my work. Trust me, it will be alright."

"I know. I need to leave. I get it, but damn Connie, $1.9 million. I won't be able to sleep for a month. Tell me something. This is your second day in here. Please tell me you found something, anything, but hopefully something good?" Giving a loud sigh he turned to walk out of the store.

"Bob."

"I know Connie, I'm leaving," as he threw his hands up in the air, seeming to have given up.

"It was an inside job, Bob." He stopped in his tracks and quickly turned back around to face Connie.

"Are you sure? It's an inside robbery by employees, really?"

Connie walked over and pointed to the security system. "Nobody could break into that, not this system, no way."

"Are you sure?"

"I'll bet you $1.9 million on it," she said with a little smile on her face. "Now all we have to do is find the right employees."

Bob looked out the door at the two policemen standing outside in the cold. "We'll get the doughnut boys on that one. Great job, Connie, great job," as he leaned over and kissed her on the cheek.

"Don't get too excited boss, they still have to catch them, and it's our job to get back the merchandise!"

"I think you just did. Look I'll call you later. I have to go."

"And where are you going, Bob?"

"I'm headed back to the police station to get someone to look into the employees working here, thanks to you, sweetheart. And hey, Connie, thanks. I'll be able to sleep tonight." And with that Bob Wesson left, grabbing a doughnut himself on his way out the door, and feeling pretty darn good about the information Connie had given him. He was off to the police station because he knew she was right, she always was.

But Connie didn't feel all that confident as she stood there alone in the most famous jewelry store in the world. She was in the middle of an investigation she was about to crack and all she could think of was her Jack. He was out there somewhere doing his thing, fighting for his country and saving lives. And here she was sifting through doughnut crumbs in search for lost diamonds.

She missed him terribly, and she also missed being in the Army. That's where she was when she met Jack Womack. For 20 years she was Military Police (MP). And for most of her years before she retired she was a part of the White House detail. Taking care of Presidents Nixon, Ford, and Carter; even the first four years of Ronald Reagan's term was on her watch. And for the last eight of those years she was the one in charge of the detail and also the first woman to ever do so.

In those days women could not serve on the battlefield. At first she had her reservations, but Connie was OK with that; she loved her job at the White House and her career as an Army officer. But she was also good, if not great, in solving crime. She had a gift when it came to putting the pieces back together and solving the unsolvable. It was Jack, her husband, that introduced her to Bob Wesson, her boss of several years now.

Jack knew she would be great as an insurance investigator solving the crimes of the stolen. From art works and jewelry to family heirlooms, Connie found it all. Bob Wesson probably knew it would be just a matter of time before some large company would scoop her up. For now Connie was happy with her second career working for Bob, but she sure missed her better-half,

Jack. Solving mysteries helped keep her mind off worrying about him a little bit, and a little was better than nothing.

Suddenly the door opened and in walked a large, good-looking man wearing a dark blue Brooks Brothers three-piece suit, and definitely looking out of place with a police badge hanging around his neck. "Hey girlfriend, found any good clues yet?" said Chris Tighe, a young thirtyish brassy but confident detective with red hair and broad shoulders. He was originally from Boston, as his accent reflected. He stood there with his hands on his hips, looking a little pissed off, Connie thought.

"No, not so far. I still have a ways to go before I have any answers, Chris, but you'll be the first to know, I promise," she said with a smile.

"First, like hell, not the way your boss tells it. It looks like I'm the last. I can see it now, tomorrow's headline reads, **The Great Connie Womack Solves Theft at Tiffany.**" Connie looked up from the blue bin. "No, Chris, that's not right. I believe it would read **No Word on Tiffany Heist.**"

"Well, what's the deal, have you solved it or not?"

"Well, as you police like to say, it will be in my report. But off the record, and I mean really off the record, Chris."

"Yeah, sure off the record, you got it, Connie."

"OK, the way I see it is there are about five people I believe who could have done it or at least knew something beforehand. I did some background checking on the employees, found a couple of things that jumped out at me. One, did you know two employees are first cousins and were best friends growing up? And one of which served two years for a four-year sentence for bank robbery.

"One's the store manager and the other employee is the one that was sentenced for bank robbery; by the way he is one of Tiffany's security guards." Detective Tighe could not believe what he was hearing as he stood there listening to Connie.

"And this security system is unbelievable, Chris. No one I know would have the knowledge to break this amazing security system. It's way too elaborate for just anyone off the street to break that code; actually, I don't know anyone that could break it. This is one hell of a security system, one of the best in the world; and we are talking Tiffany here. And here's the kicker, the lay-out, someone would have had the blueprints of the jewelry cases to do it the way it was done."

She walked over to one of the kiosks. "Look Chris, these guys went straight to the good stuff," as she pointed to the broken kiosks throughout the store. "See these diamonds they missed? The reason is because they're fakes, and subsequently were not touched, but where the real diamonds were that's where you see broken kiosks. Someone had to know the difference between the two."

"Inside job, that's what you are saying." Chris Tighe leaned back on one of the jewelry cases and pondered Connie's analysis. Then he repeated himself. "Inside job you're sure?" He rubbed his hand over his mouth and red mustache as he was thinking.

"I would bet the farm, boyfriend, the whole thing, lock, stock, and the old barrel too."

"Store manager?"

"I spoke to him this morning. He acted pretty solid but if I were you, I sure would talk to him while he is still in the country, but my answer on an inside job is yes, that's what I think. But after saying all of that, I would certainly start with the ex-con cousin of his, he'll break faster. Heck, I thought he was going to confess when I first spoke to him."

Detective Chris Tighe shook his head knowing she was probably right. She always was. "Connie you are the best and on the behalf of the New York police department, thank you for your service and hard work. In gratitude, let me buy you a drink across the street. What do you say, lady?"

'That's sweet, Chris, but I'm on my way to LaGuardia. I have to catch the shuttle to DC tonight. Say, how about a rain check, maybe next time, handsome." She leaned over and gave him a friendly kiss on the cheek.

"Connie, you are one fine lady and a great detective." He returned the affection with a hug. "Be safe in your travels, Connie, and I hope to see you soon and again thanks." He then turned back around to face her. "By the way my men will help you with those boxes of evidence whenever you're ready."

Chris then turned and walked out the door. He stopped and talked to the two doughnut cops and then got in his car and drove off. Connie put all the evidence in the plastic containers and sealed them with bright yellow tape so they could not be opened without breaking the tape. She then walked over and tapped on the glass.

The doughnut cops looked up as she motioned for them to come inside. Once they were inside Connie explained what they needed to do with the evidence and to be careful that nothing showed up missing once they made it to the precinct's evidence room. She then got her personal belongings, took a couple of laps around the store to make sure she did not miss anything, and headed to the door. She stopped just before she exited and turned back around toward the policemen. She could not help but get in one last jab at those two.

"Please men, please be careful. If you do a good job there's a doughnut in it for you!" With that she left with a smile on her face.

Bad, Bad Baghdad

Chapter 4

THE DESERT SANDS BLEW HARD AS JACK Womack landed several miles off course, outside of the city of Baghdad. By himself and totally in the dark, he soon acclimated to his surroundings as he cut on his night-vision glasses and proceeded to quickly gather up his black parachute. He found a nearby drainage ditch where he threw the parachute and covered it with sand and rocks. He promptly checked and inventoried his equipment and rechecked his weapons.

Everything seemed to have made the drop as he checked his GPS, the newest toy he had in his arsenal. He knew exactly where he was or, in this case, where he wasn't. He wasn't where he was supposed to be, as he rechecked his location once again on the GPS. *They didn't figure on the wind being this strong,* he guessed, but whatever the case Jack Womack was a good two if not three miles off course. And there was no way he could risk breaking radio silence.

He would just have to walk and make up the difference. Maybe the others were off target as well. It was a good chance they were, he thought, as he plotted his course and studied his maps. It looked as if he was in better shape than he first thought. Jack grabbed his watch and started pressing a button on the side, making a series of dots and dashes. He then stopped and waited for a reply. Quickly more dots and dashes came across his watch as Jack read the primitive Morse code, still effective in times of need. It was from Rhys. It seemed everyone was off course as Jack had guessed.

"C-P-W-UD-L....H-T" Jack typed the letters meaning words out on his watch, (change of plan . . . will update later . . . headed to target). That was the second location if something was to go wrong with the first, as it did. The Euphrates River was the team's second choice but it turned out they were too far from it as well. They were not too far from the town of Fallujah, which was only a few miles outside of Baghdad International Airport off highway A-14.

The TARGET Jack was referring to was the Al-Faw Palace, and that was their final destination. It was known as the Water Palace and the primary home of Saddam Hussein although it was built more like a fort. The palace was located just five kilometers from the airport, their planned escape route, but by the way things were going that had a good chance to change as well.

Rhys typed back 10-4, (roger that) and Jack was headed off to the other preplanned rendezvous point. As he checked the time on his watch he looked up at the night sky. He knew he only had about two hours to make it to the rendezvous point before the sun would be up, and so would his cover, and in a Muslim country everyone would be up at dawn to meet the rising sun.

To his right Jack could see and hear the bombs exploding over Baghdad in the distance. The aerial assault was quite a sight as Jack made his way up the road hiding behind anything and everything he could find whenever he saw people or headlights of a vehicle approaching. Jack watched as a line of M-35 troop carriers, a truck known to most soldiers as a Deuce and a Half, approached. Truck after truck roared by loaded with the Republican Guard, Hussein's elite soldiers. They were fleeing the burning city of Baghdad headed out towards the desert and Fallujah, which was only 68 kilometers from Baghdad.

Rhys was lucky that he met up with most of his men as soon as he landed, but they too were more west from the drop site than they first believed. Rhys saw a light flash twice, then two more times. He knew it was coming from one of his men as he heard a voice call out.

"Lieutenant Garret, over here," called out 2nd class Petty Officer Phil Owens, nicknamed Oil Can. He was called Oil Can because he loved to work on cars. Phil could make anything with a motor run, plus he used Vitalis on his hair. He was the best explosive expert Rhys and Jack knew, but he was still just a good old southern boy from Savannah, Georgia, and really down to earth.

The other Navy SEAL member was Randall Remick, nicknamed Recoil. He thought all the ladies loved him, and most of them did. He and Phil were the oldest in the outfit. The Delta Force guys out of Fort Bragg, North Carolina, were Steven Hyatt, code name Hotel, and Raymond Putnam, known as Rain Man, not because he loved the movie that had just come out, but he was great with dates and numbers. He could remember anything. Those two guys were best of friends and both had grown up together in Florence, South Carolina. As single soldiers they both were really good but together they made one hell of a killing machine.

Rhys had all of them check their gear one more time to see if it made the trip down. He waited a couple of minutes to see if the other two rookies made it, both Army Rangers out of Fort Bragg. The big tall one was a Lumbee Native American named Cecil Locklear. Everyone called him Chief. The other Ranger was Thomas Wise from Lockport, New York, upstate, right outside of Niagara Falls. His nickname was Skeeter, because he hated mosquitoes. Wherever he was, if there were mosquitoes within miles of him they would find him and eat him up, thus his hatred of mosquitoes. Skeeter seemed to be the gambler in the group, always betting on anything and everything. His nickname probably should have been Vegas.

Rhys could not wait any longer on the rookies. He yelled, "All right guys, let's move out," as his patience had run out. He called the group to muster up their gear once again as they headed out in search of their commander, Jack Womack. They stayed mainly to the sides of the roads. Their brown and sandy colored uniforms camouflaged them to a point, but in the great wide open as they were only the darkness of night covered their location. Rhys knew that the darkness, too, would soon be gone as they marched on into the night.

Out of the blue came an explosion, then another, as the men jumped for cover. The sounds of gunfire rang out in the distance. Rhys and the men heard the sound of a vehicle, an M-35 troop transport, as it pulled up right in front of the five men. The driver stopped, apparently for no particular reason, as he spoke on the radio. He never saw Rhys and his men as his conversation quickly ended but he did not move.

The driver let a couple of minutes go by, as if he was waiting for more cargo, more troops, more something. Rhys motioned with his hand as he ran his finger across his throat to Rain Man and Hotel Steve and without a word the two men crawled under the passenger side of the vehicle and disappeared underneath. Rhys and the others watched but saw no sign of the two. A few seconds passed before the onlookers saw the Iraqi soldier collapse in the front seat as the two Delta guys seized the truck and signaled for the rest to climb aboard. Quickly they all scrambled and jumped in the back of the covered truck. Rhys reached once again for his watch to send a message to Jack.

At the same time Chief and Skeeter finally caught up with the rest of the team, but Chief stopped in the dark just short of where the team could see them. Standing in the shadows Chief grabbed Skeeter by the arm and gave him a stern look, as he softly whispered in Skeeter's ear. "Remember don't you say a word about where we've been," as he pointed to the piece of paper tucked in his shirt. "You fucken understand me boy?" Skeeter shook his head in the affirmative. They both then continued to walk out of the darkness directly behind the truck.

"Hey hold it fellows, it's us!" The voices in the dark startled all five men in the vehicle. They quickly jumped in the direction of the sound, with all five guns pointing at Chief and Skeeter.

"Hold it, hold it, damn it, Lieutenant Garret it's us," in a whispered shout said Chief, as the two stood there like prisoners with their hands up in the air.

"Hold your fire men, damn you two, hold your fire," said Rhys as he repeated himself, making sure everyone finally realized who the surprise guests were. They lowered their pointed guns down to the floor of the vehicle.

"Son of bitches, you two rookies are going to be the death of me. Where the hell have you two been and where are your headsets? I tried Morse code, but we couldn't reach you on the radio watches or anything."

Neither one said a word other than sorry. "Damn boys, we were about to leave your asses." Again, there was nothing but silence from the two stragglers. As time was becoming more of a factor Rhys decided to overlook the matter and write it off as two dumb-ass rookies. "Oh hell, hurry up and get your asses in the truck before we shoot you two!"

As the two men climbed into the truck, Rhys hit the cab of the truck with his fist and Rain Man threw the truck in gear and drove off. Rhys, still not convinced of why they were late, asked a few more questions as the truck drove down the road closer to the airport.

"Now where the hell have you two been? We have been waiting on you all night it seems like."

Chief was the one that did all the talking. "Sir, yes sir, well you see the wind must have blown us off course by a mile or two. We're lucky as hell we two found each other boss," as Chief pointed his finger at specialist Wise. "Hell, I landed on a damn house or building of some kind and Skeeter there, hell he was lying in the street below me. We had a hell of a hard time making it to this place I can tell you that. We got lost about a hundred times but anyway we made it, sir."

"Yes sir, we made it," echoed Skeeter looking pretty wild-eyed himself. Chief looked over at him as if he was saying shut the hell up.

"You got lost? Your GPS not working either?" Again, not one word from those two, just a shoulder shrug. Rhys stopped his interrogation, knowing those two were not going to say shit regardless of what he asked them. "Well, thank God that's all that has happened so far," said Rhys as he turned toward the cab of the truck and knocked a couple of times getting Hotel Steve's attention. He handed him a map through the back window. Rhys pointed to the red dot marked on the map. "Here, right here, this is where we're going, OK?"

"Yes sir, we got it sir." Hotel pointed out to Rain Man the airport sign up ahead. Rain Man slowed the truck to take the right turn up ahead and then next left as they merged out onto the highway. It was just like driving back home, they thought. But this wasn't I-95 in Florence, South Carolina, headed south to Florida. No this was Baghdad, Iraq, and they were headed for the Al-Faw Palace just outside of the Iraqi International Airport. The first order of business was to pick up Jack along the way.

Skeeter looked over at Chief with a smile on his face that he could not wash off. Chief looked back over at Skeeter and nonchalantly placed a finger to his lips as if to say be quiet. Rhys noticed the two acting strangely and began to wonder what those two had been up to. Something was not right. The two went missing way too long and without any communication. Chief stared back at the Lieutenant but gave no indication that anything was amiss. Rhys had digressed, the mission came first, and the first thing he needed to do was get back in contact with Jack. Through all the dealings with those two Rhys had forgotten to message Jack back, as he reached for the button on the side of the watch and started to type.

"Have all in tow—on way-give us signal when eyes on." Rhys finished his messaging and sat back for the ride, but very soon his rest was interrupted when out of nowhere two Iraqi Willis Jeeps, vintage 1945, pulled directly in behind their truck.

"Boss, we got company," shouted Rain Man as the headlights filled his side view mirrors.

"Keep cool everybody, stay calm and move back here closer to the cab," said Rhys as he pulled out a couple of hand-grenades and waited. Then a voice over a loud speaker from one of the jeeps blurted out something in Arabic. As one jeep tried to pass the Deuce and a Half Rain Man sped up trying to stop their advancement. Once again the voice came over the loudspeaker as the second jeep pulled up alongside the truck. Like rush hour in Atlanta, all three vehicles were side by side and moving at a high rate of speed.

"Enough of this shit! Let's bust their asses." Rhys signaled to Recoil to answer with a volley of gunfire. Both jeeps quickly pulled back behind the troop carrier as gunfire rang out both sides of the truck. Recoil, Chief, and Phil moved from the sides and repositioned themselves, this time aiming out the back of the truck. Rhys shouted, "Hit 'em again," as all five men unloaded on the two old Willis Jeeps as they were right in their sights.

Shooting out all four headlights and a windshield caused the two vehicles to swing to the outside of the truck avoiding more gunfire. Quickly they regrouped and soon were back and approaching from the rear of the truck once more. "Haul ass," Rhys shouted to Rain Man, who floored the gas pedal. Chief and Oilcan returned more fire but the two bullet-riddled Iraqi jeeps still advanced and were right on their tails. Return fire kept raining bullets in the back of the truck as they were taking heavy fire from the two Browning .50 caliber machine guns that were mounted on the two jeeps, looking like an episode straight out of the old TV show "Rat Patrol."

"Get down, drop to the floor men," Rhys shouted as he pulled the pins on two grenades and started his count to two before he threw them at the same time. Each grenade exploded as each bounced once off the hoods of the two vehicles. The explosions caused one jeep to hit the other as both flaming vehicles wrecked in the middle of the empty highway, leaving them lying on their sides to burn. Jack's men cheered at the explosions and the carnage on the street but not Rhys. He knew the worst had just happened. Their cover was blown. And Jack was going to be upset to say the least. "Everyone OK?" Rhys asked, as everyone checked to see if everyone survived the gunfire. And indeed they had. Everyone was OK. Then they felt the truck slowing down.

"We got more company boss, looks like an LMV," shouted Rain Man, as Rhys looked down the road and saw the Iveco LMVs (Light Multirole Vehicles) parked in the highway blocking their passage.

Hotel Steve looked at Rain Man. "You know those LMVs are like small tanks. You don't want no part of them."

"No shit, Sherlock," replied his Buddy, as he shouted back to Rhys. "Where to boss?"

"Looks like we are going cross-country boys so hold on to something tight. Rain Man take a hard right now, and again right here! Now cut through there," Rhys shouted as he pointed to open desert. On demand and without hesitation Rain Man quickly turned the large troop carrier off the flat and smooth interstate-type highway onto the rough and unknowing desert terrain as shots once again rang out. The soldiers held on tight as the truck rammed through small rock walls, ditches, and even clipped a corner or two on a few buildings and houses. Rhys kept looking back but never saw any headlights. He could not believe they didn't make chase. Finally they found a small road which led them to where the airport was in sight.

Rhys pulled out the radio and called up Jack. "Captain Crunch to Cracker Jack, come in Cracker Jack." Rhys worked the radio trying to make the signal stronger. The rest of the men looked over at each other and mouthed the words Captain Crunch and Cracker Jack, as they all thought how lame that sounded. O-C looked over at Recoil as to say, "what the hell, Cracker Jack?" The men laughed a little but didn't dare do it in front of Rhys.

The long-awaited reply came. "Cracker Jack to Captain Crunch, here. Over."

"That's him," Rhys shouted as he looked in the cab of the truck. "Ray, where the hell are we?" he asked.

"Sir, we are on Al Zaytoon Street. Right there's Baghdad University believe it or not, and beside it is the College of Agriculture. Right there is highway 11," as he pointed to the road signs.

And sure enough they were sitting right beside Baghdad U. The radio crackled back alive as Jack gave up his position. "Eyes on Captain Crunch, want some coffee, boys?" as a flashlight suddenly blinked two times. Its direction was down the street from where they were parked and appeared to be coming from the coffee shop on the corner.

"Hey, look over there," shouted Hotel Steve as he pointed to the sign down the street to the left. And there it was, sure enough, in purple and white neon a sign written in English, **THE STUDENT CLUB COFFEE SHOP**, flashing on and off and bigger than life.

"Let's roll" ordered Rhys as the Deuce and a Half roared back to life. They drove right in front of the University of Baghdad, and two blocks later they picked up Commander Jack Womack who was standing on the street corner at the students' coffee shop. The air brakes sounded as the Army truck paused for a second, long enough for Jack to climb aboard as he jumped in the back of the truck to hitch a ride. The truck then quickly disappeared, turning down a narrow side street to hide from view of the highway. Cheers went up as his men greeted Jack with handshakes and pats on the back. They all seemed genuinely glad to see him safe.

"Man, it's great to see you guys. Now let's ditch the truck ASAP. Our target is right down the street." He looked over at Rhys for an update.

"Sir everyone made it to this point safe and sound, so far," he stated.

"Any problems getting here? Did anyone see you?"

Rhys hung his head down a little. "Sir, yes sir, I'm afraid we woke up the natives. They know we're here, sir. We took out a couple of jeeps and had to deal with an LMV or two. But we made it this far and we are ready for our mission sir."

"Sounds good. Hey, Rain Man, drive over toward that direction. I want to get as close to the airport as possible without being seen. You copy that?" Ray acknowledged with a nod. "I want to be in that palace as soon as we can."

"Roger that boss, I'm on it." He and Hotel Steve looked over at the map and the GPS to get the right coordinates so they could plot a new course, this time heading straight to the target. Jack and the rest of his crew sat back and enjoyed the ride as if they were taking in a Sunday afternoon drive back home. Ray pulled the steering wheel left and right zigzagging back and forth, passing abandoned cars that dotted the streets due north of the city on route to the Al-Faw Palace and their main target, Saddam Hussein himself.

Enough School

Chapter 5

CONNIE HAD THE BARTENDER POUR HER ANOTHER ONE of her favorite drinks, vodka tonic with a lime twist in a tall glass, as she waited for her best friend Kay. They had not seen each other in months. They both mainly lived in Washington but with Connie's business causing her to travel so much and with Kay still in school getting numerous doctorate degrees all over the place it was hard for the two to get together. Nevertheless, Connie always tried to see Kay when she was in town and this trip was no different.

"Here you go pretty lady." The bartender placed a coaster under Connie's newest libation. The noise from the table around the corner grew as several more people arrived. After a few minutes Connie turned toward the sound. "Boy they must be having a good time," said the bartender.

Connie thought the same as the noise was about to get on her last nerve, being that it was only 4:30 in the afternoon. Finally the noise subsided as a good-looking young lady stood up and announced to the whole restaurant she was going to the bathroom and to hold her spot as she pointed to the area between two of the four young men at the loud table. Connie spotted her as she walked around the bar, but the lady was too drunk to notice Connie. She had one mission and that was strictly making it to the bathroom before a problem arose.

"Well, hey there girlfriend, having a good time, are we?" Connie said to the young lady who was walking past the bar and without a question was totally wasted. She then suddenly stopped after recognizing the voice as if she was balancing on a tightrope with one half of her body still going forward and the rest in reverse. She stood there blinking in slow motion as she tried to focus on both the face and voice talking to her. After a couple of seconds went by she shouted and threw her arms around Connie, which helped her stand up better as she held on for dear life.

"Woo-mack, when did you get here," she said with a thick tongue and forgetting they were supposed to meet. She stopped and turned towards the bar using it as a hand rail for her balance.

"Hello Kay, having a good time, are we?"

"Connie," she shouted again. "I passed! I'm board certified! I'm a doctor of psychiatry now," she exclaimed as she fell back into Connie's arms.

Connie was feeling a little uncomfortable holding up her best friend. "Well that's great but you need to stand up there Sigmund Freud and stop making a scene. Kay, get a grip now, please stand up straighter, you need to get yourself together, Kay, damn it."

The smile suddenly left Kay's face. "I don't feel too good." Connie quickly realized the next stop her girlfriend needed was the restroom. As the two wrestled each other up and off Connie's bar stool, Connie grabbed Kay's arm, helping her down the long line of bar stools and barely making it to the bathroom in time. Kay tried to grab the doorknob as Connie came to the rescue and helped her open the door to the stall, and quickly down on her knees Kay went as soon as the door opened. She grabbed the steering wheel to the porcelain bus and waited for the long bumpy ride. Connie stood out by the sinks thinking of how great this night was going to be after she got Freud off the toilet, poor girl.

And there she was just graduated with a doctorate degree in psychiatry having a prayer meeting for one, as she sat spread-eagled on the tile floor of the ladies' bathroom. This was the same girl who was first in her class at Georgetown. She then spent only three years, not four or five like most, before she got her MD degree at Georgetown.

As long as Connie could remember Kay always wanted to be a psychiatrist. She wanted it so bad plus she loved it, and one would have to, after spending all the time and money she did. It took her two more years to receive her Doctor of Osteopathic Medicine degree at the University of Maryland, not to mention the two or three years of biomedical, clinical sciences, and two years of core clinical training she received from the prestigious Perelman school of Medicine at the University of Pennsylvania in Philadelphia. That's where she did her four years of residency before taking the specialty board examination for board certification.

Connie stood there and thought about how many years this girl who was lying on the bathroom floor throwing-up had spent on education, and obviously it was not enough. It had to have been at least 12 if not 14 years. But that was Connie's buddy, and not just buddies but best friends, and had been through all the ups and downs of adolescent years and high school as they grew up in the same neighborhood.

This was her very best friend through thick and thin, and somehow they were going to get through this as well, they always did, she thought. But how would she get Kay out of this bathroom? She surely was not able to lift her body weight. Connie thought a few moments till the answer arrived. Those assholes, she thought, that's the answer. She knew Kay wasn't going anywhere as Connie marched out of the bathroom and headed to the table of four.

"Bartender, call me a cab," she said as she walked by him on her way to the table.

"You're a cab," he replied, and a couple of customers laughed. She turned her head and stuck out her tongue.

"You're a funny man, yeah look no tip for you," she said as she kept walking till she rounded the corner where she suddenly stopped at the booth of four. Shot glasses and empty beer pitchers covered the table top. Connie stared and could not help but notice that these guys were hammered.

"Well, hey there good looking. Can we help you with something, maybe buy you a drink or ten?" said one of the four preppy college age kids sitting at the same table where Kay had been earlier.

"No, I'm good, but I do have a question," as she pulled out her old military police badge and flashed it in front of the four long faces. They were too drunk to realize the badge she was holding was her old Marine MP shield when she was in the military, plus she flashed it in their faces too fast for anyone to really read it anyway. "Can't you four assholes read? Better still, I'm here to check your IDs. And to find out which one of you got an underage girl who is now throwing up in the women's bathroom really drunk. That's why I'm over here. There surely isn't a person man enough at this table for me! Now let's see those IDs boys?"

"Now wait a minute, lady, we didn't know she was underage," one said. "Hell, she looked older than us."

Another guy spoke up. "Wait a minute sweetheart. We go to Georgetown University. You don't have a right to come in and question us about drinking," said the one sitting by the empty seat where Kay had been. He quickly got her attention with that tone of voice that really pissed off Connie.

"I said IDs," as the men slowly removed them from their billfolds and laid them on the table. Connie picked up the one from the smart mouth and read it. "Well, Brad, looks like you boys are going downtown and spend the night in jail on the taxpayers of the Virginia Commonwealth. Now get your ass up," Connie shouted.

"Excuse me lady but we go to school right there in Washington, DC, where the drinking age is 18," as he pointed across the street at the school.

"Well, that's all fine and good and I'm sure you four are smart men, if you are going to Georgetown and all, but you see smartass, you're not in Washington city limits. Your ass is across the street in the great state of Virginia where the drinking age is 21. Now I said get up."

"Wait a minute, lady, we didn't know. Please don't put us in jail. We'll do anything. Please, our parents will kill us, please not jail." The whole gang was crying like babies. Connie could not stand it. She was about to cry herself.

"Hold it, shut-up, I said hold it. Look here then, if you help me this one time I'll let you off the hook, but you will have to promise me you'll quit drinking in this bar and turn yourselves in at the police station."

"What? Turn ourselves in? Are you crazy, lady?" one said.

But the other three agreed, "Yes ma'am, anything, you just name it. Anything, yes ma'am what do you need?"

"Follow me," as Connie and her captives marched out from the table around the corner of the bar and to the ladies' bathroom. Connie knocked on the door and looked over at the four. "You four wait right here," as she stepped into the bathroom doorway.

"Hey lady your cab is here," shouted the bartender. Connie ignored him and went straight inside to check on Kay. To her surprise Kay was standing at the sinks but leaning on the wall as she applied some makeup. Still drunk but handling it very well, Connie thought to herself.

"Did you get their asses?" Kay asked as she applied her lipstick, perfectly.

"I got 'em alright, I got all four out front now, standing on the other side of this door, and our cab is outside waiting."

"OK, then give me a second," as Kay got down and lay on the floor, pulling down on her dress, making sure her underwear was covered up. "Go ahead, let them in."

Connie opened the door on cue. "Alright there's nobody else is in here." She then motioned with her hands for the guys to come inside to get Kay. "Now you be careful helping her up, you hear me?" The four guys slowly and carefully lifted her up and carried her out of the bathroom with her feet dragging the floor. She looked like she had been knocked out. They then took her out through the front door and placed her in the waiting cab. One guy handed the cabbie forty bucks. Connie got inside beside Kay and rolled down the window. And just before the cab drove off Kay sat up in the cab and looked at all four.

"Hey boys, next time try harder if you want to get a girl really drunk, or better still, go fuck yourselves," shouted Kay as she sat up in the seat and gave those four the middle finger as the cab drove off. The two friends settled back in the seat of the cab laughing.

Kay turned to her best friend and grabbed Connie's hand, the smile gone from her face. "Mother died last week. I was going to tell you but she did not want a service. I have her ashes at home." A tear ran down her face.

"I'm so sorry, Kay." Connie knew something else had to be wrong for her to get that drunk, that early. She then leaned over and with a hug tried to console her best friend.

"I'm so glad you are here with me now," said Kay as the two friends embraced with a hug. The rest of the ride was pretty quiet. The two sat in the back seat of the cab with their thoughts mainly on Mrs. Shirley and what a fine and fun person she had been, always the life of any party, always a fun and outgoing personality, much like her daughter. As evening came that night the two girls sat together reliving their childhood, remembering great times by telling old stories of both families. They tried to catch up on good times, old memories, and bad boyfriends, laughing and enjoying their friendship, knowing it would last forever.

Hussein's Al-Faw Palace

Chapter 6

EVERYONE WAITED FOR THE ORDER TO BE GIVEN as they lay in the dirt just beyond the huge concrete walls and several rows of barbwire fencing that encircled the royal palace. This was Al-Faw, the palace of the waters; one of over 90 homes and palaces of President Saddam Hussein Abd al-Majid al-Tikriti. But this one was special and considered to be his favorite.

The home was fitted with over 60 rooms and 29 bathrooms.

Two days earlier recon had shown it to be heavily guarded with Saddam Hussein's elite Army, the Republican Guard. The palace was also known to house Hussein's sons, Uday and Qusay, who used the place as a sexual playground as well as an elaborate torture chamber. The lake surrounding the home was used for recreation as they spent days jet and water skiing and partying all night. Thousands of army soldiers used the palace like a state-owned resort, pampering themselves with their own vision of R&R before going back into combat against Iran which had been going on for years.

But Jack and his men saw no one relaxing or swimming, or even fishing. Of course it was still night but the fact was they saw no one in sight. This puzzled Jack, causing him to order two lookouts as he pointed to Chief and Skeeter. Without hesitation they grabbed their gear and the two sprinted off, climbing over a small fence and down into a small drainage ditch. They were hoping to keep their presence undetected by the enemy as they moved down and across the long two-lane bridge that separated the island palace from the mainland. After a few minutes Jack signaled to Hotel Steve and Ray that it was time for them to advance. They also were quickly up and over the wall, and in a flash they were out on their own recon mission. Watching them go, Jack knew that something still didn't feel right. He looked across the large lake waiting for something to happen and it didn't. Rhys sensed it as well.

"I'm thinking it's a trap, Jack," said Rhys while looking through his NVGs trying to assess the situation.

"Well, our recon information sucks, that's one thing for sure," Jack said as he looked back over the wall for a second glance. "There's no one home. The damn place appears to be totally empty. I don't get it, Rhys; 48 hours ago this place was full of tanks, trucks, and over 1,500 elite soldiers. Now there's hardly a light on and if it wasn't for the wind there would be hardly any movement of any kind. I thought the recon was good, but this place looks like no one has been here for days, I just don't get it."

Abruptly Jack jumped as he and Rhys saw a light that appeared to be coming from the main entrance of the palace. They both watched and studied the landscape as the two large gates in front of the palace slowly opened. They located the light directly in the front of the palace. Rain Man and Hotel had just moved into position when the wrought iron gates started to open but they stayed back in the dark, noticing that it was a young lady holding a flashlight. Standing beside her looked to be an older man. They both stood at the front door opening, as if they knew someone was out there. It appeared to be a white handkerchief or cloth in her hand, but before anyone could say a thing two shots rang out and the two civilians dropped to the ground.

"Holy shit where did those shots come from," shouted Jack as he scanned the front of the palace, then removed his NVGs and looked over at Rhys for an answer he didn't have. But before he could say a word two more shots ring out, then silence.

"Hotel, you want to tell me what the hell is going on up there?" Jack asked through his headset.

Hotel replied in a soft voice, "Beats the shit out of me, sir. Four shots fired all coming from the right of us, sir, it was not us."

"Chief, what say you? Chief, come in Chief. Skeeter? Chief, damn it, someone answer me, damn it!" Jack looked over at one of his most seasoned of the lot and probably his best fighter, Petty Officer first class Phil Owens who was a Navy SEAL himself and someone Jack could trust with his life. "Oilcan, you and Recoil get your asses up there and be my eyes." He then called back to Steve Hyatt on the microphone. "Hotel, hold your position, got two more headed your way."

Oilcan looked at Jack. "Yes sir, boss, we're on it, come on RC let's check it out." And the two were off and over the wall in two seconds.

"Boss we got two civilians down at the front door, one a young girl appears to be holding a white flag," said Hotel as he and Rain Man made their way into the palace.

"I said to hold up."

"Sorry boss, we ran inside when we heard the second round of shooting, and boss there is no one here. This place looks as empty as an Egyptian tomb."

"Roger that Rain Man. Oilcan is headed your way. See if you can find Chief and Skeeter, over."

"Will do boss, over and out."

Jack sat down behind the wall and removed his NVGs and took a deep breath. "Damn, Rhys, this thing is messed up, big time. What the hell is going on up there?"

"I don't know, boss, but it looks like a couple of guys are not on the same page with the rest of the team, boss."

"What do you think is wrong with those two and especially with Chief? Something has to be done to rein him in."

"Boss he wasn't right at the drop site. We waited a long time for those two and by the time he and Wise did show up they weren't acting right at all. They were smiling and laughing, like they just left a party or something. If we had needed to wait two more minutes we would have left their asses. I can't put my finger on it but trust me, they were up to something."

"Chief, come in, over," Jack called on his microphone, but still no answer.

Rain Man and Steve waited inside the doorway of the palace, their eyes covering every square inch of the front of the compound. They both quickly turned to the right as they heard another shot fired. Hotel called for instructions. "Boss we heard more shots, request permission to advance and investigate."

"Roger that, Hotel. Proceed with caution and check your six," he replied.

"Sir, yes sir," answered Hotel as he and Ray slowly moved forward through the large foyer. Once inside the rotunda they looked up and saw a huge dome about 15 stories tall, and the room itself appeared to be about the size of an average putting green about 5,000 square feet. And throughout the room hung fake copies of famous paintings like Leonardo da Vinci's the *Mona Lisa* and others by Claude Monet, which dotted the otherwise bare walls. Bare rooms for that matter, hardly any furniture covered the floor in the massive room, but Ray was thinking more like they were sitting ducks if they had to take cover.

Slowly they worked their way across the giant open room and headed in the direction of the last gunshot which seemed to have come from down the same long hallway they were now standing in front of. Beads of sweat ran down their faces, partly due to nerves, but mainly because of the heat. There was no air moving, no air conditioning, no fans, all of which was making it really hot. Hotel Steve and Ray cautiously rechecked their ammo and firearms, then began to make their way down the dark hall.

After several hundred feet they made it to a large downward flight of stairs which led them down two long golden-colored corridors that opened up into another huge room. Each room was full of famous oil paintings as well, from Rembrandt to Picasso, and large chandeliers dotted the cathedral ceiling overhead, but still they saw no one. It was a like a ghost town as the two specialists worked their way down another hallway that opened to several bedrooms.

Hotel Steve took one side of the hall and Ray took the other as they both darted their heads inside each room one by one checking for any occupants. Their search carried them deep and far into the palace but regardless of how far and how many rooms their travels took them each room still came up empty. They were getting more frustrated by the minute.

"You know Steve, there's only 69 of these damn rooms in this place." Steve then promptly stopped without warning as his eye caught the glimmer of a light he saw coming from one of the back bedrooms.

"Shut-up, Ray, look over there," Steve whispered as he put his finger to his lips and pointed to a light that was shining around the doorframe to one of the smaller back rooms. Slowly each man continued to search, heading in the direction of the light. Ray started feeling a little more uncomfortable at this point and signaled to stop to rest for a minute. He knew that being this far away from the others and deep in the heart of a madman's domicile was not a good place to be. Ray looked at Steve as he pulled on the back of his shirt to get his attention.

"What the hell are we doing in here, Steve?" Ray asked.

"Shut-up," he replied again in a whisper, "can't you hear that?" as noises were heard coming from behind the small door in the back of the room. They walked cautiously toward the corner of the dimly lit room and closer till the two were standing directly in front of a closet of some kind.

"We are doing our job, Ray, now come on," as the two advanced up to a small door and Steve slowly turned the knob. The light glowed around them as the door was slowly opened. The noise of voices was clearly being heard on the other side as the two stepped through the small door opening and inside where stairs led them down to a large basement.

The further they went down the steps the more clearly they could hear the voices, real familiar voices. Steve raised his fist as they stopped before they would be seen. Without a doubt it was Cecil, aka Chief, who was doing the shouting. Steve craned his neck around the corner of the stairway enough to see down into a basement. It had to be one of Uday and Qusay Hussein's torture chambers, full of what looked like barbaric exercising equipment with chains with shackles attached to the floor, and they were attached all along the gray concrete walls as well. Steve then turned his head where he now could see both Skeeter and Chief, plus a third man who was tied to a chair and was completely covered in blood. Blood covered the basement floor at his feet as well. Chief was standing over him pointing a large knife at him as he spoke.

"Alright damn you, I know you understand me damn it! Now for the last time, where is the gold? I know you people have truckloads of the stuff, now where is it, you Dune-coon, son of a bitch?" The man let out a scream as Chief not only stabbed him but was sticking the knife in and twisting it into the man's side as more blood started pouring out of his broken body and down his left leg. Steve and Ray did not know what to do as they both backed up off the steps and just looked at each other.

Steve decided to call the commander for backup using Morse code so he would not be heard. As he started to send the message they could hear the screams and cries of the man being tortured. Steve kept sending his message as he tapped softly on the microphone in his headset. "Hotel, got a situation with Chief and Skeeter requesting assistance. Muster on our GPS coordinates?"

Jack and Rhys were still outside of the palace waiting to hear from anyone when Steve's message came over his headset. Jack quickly sat up and hit Rhys on his arm when the transmission dot by dot came through.

"It's Hotel," he said to Rhys. He then replied back to Steve and Ray in a soft voice. "Roger that Hotel, hold tight, help is on the way." Jack turned back to Rhys. "You were right, something was up with those two assholes." Jack called everyone else's headset but Chief's and Skeeter's. "Everyone meet on Hotel's GPS. We're going in." After that he and Rhys left their positions behind the wall and headed out for the Al-Faw Palace. Oilcan and Recoil heard the message and quickly headed in Hotel's direction for back up.

Ray and Steve could still hear Chief demanding answers. "I said where the hell are the trucks carrying the gold?" but this time, out of pure anger, he stretched out and stabbed the man deep into his chest a couple of times as the man's screams seemed to be more intense this time and really loud.

"What the hell, we can't just let this man die, Steve, what the fuck," said Ray as he turned back to the stairs and started down to the basement. Hotel Steve waited on the steps as Rain Man eased his way down the stairs to get closer and to confront both Chief and Skeeter.

"OK, Chief, that's enough. Now let's back the fuck up!"

Cecil was at first startled as he quickly turned to face the sound of Ray's voice. "Where the hell did you come from, Rain Man?"

"How's about putting that butcher knife down right there, big man, and no one will get hurt, and you too asshole," shouted Ray as he looked over at Skeeter. Sweat was pouring down Ray's face as he stood there with his gun pointed at his two team members who were United States Army Rangers. Both men looked surprised knowing they were caught red-handed.

"Rain Man! Damn it boy, you scared the shit out of me. At first I thought you were the enemy," said Chief. "Man it's good to see another Carolina boy down here, but you can put down that weapon now. We are on the same side, remember?" Ray didn't budge, and Chief kept talking but he never dropped his knife as he placed his hand on his gun as if he was ready to shoot.

"I said to back the fuck up, Chief, and drop your gun and that big-ass knife." Moving slowly, Chief dropped the knife and threw the gun on the floor. "Now raise your arms over your head and put both hands on the back of your head, NOW," Ray shouted.

"Rain Man it's cool, brother, we were just getting some information out of the prisoner here. Hell man, there ain't nobody in here brother. We got this place to ourselves," said Chief as he backed up a couple of feet away from both the bleeding prisoner and Ray.

"That's not the way we interrogate anybody, much less shooting an innocent child and an old man like you two did on the front steps of this house, you sons of bitches."

"Now, now, Ray, aren't you being a little judgmental. Hell, we didn't kill anyone. Shit man, we are no different than you and that partner of yours, old Hotel Steve. Buddy, we are here to do a job and that's what we were trying to do before you came down those stairs. Now why don't you two turn around and go back and tell little old Commander Womack and his butt-buddy Lieutenant Garret that everything is fine and dandy. And act like you tried but you two could not find Skeeter or little ol' me. Hell, I'll mark this down as a learning experience for you two old homeboys."

"Chief you know if they tell, we got to kill 'em too," shouted Skeeter with his arms in the air as well.

"No, heck everything is good with me and my man Ray here. Shoot we are from the same part of the country, Carolina boys stick together ain't that right, Ray?"

The whole time Cecil was talking Steve had a bead on him with his gun ready to fire, as he sat on the steps just out of Cecil's view. Ray knew his Delta member had his back and also knew Jack would send more backup by now and all they had to do is wait this thing out, knowing the cavalry was coming.

"No Chief, I think we will wait this one out. Now, both of you on the floor and kick your guns over here. Steve, get your butt down here and help me with these two assholes." Steve hated giving away his position, but he reluctantly came down with his gun pointing at Cecil's head.

"Hey, fellas, killed anybody lately?" Cecil didn't say a word. He was not surprised. He knew Steve had to be close-by. Those two did everything together and he knew it.

More sounds of pain started coming from the prisoner. He was bleeding pretty badly at this point; his whole left side was covered in blood as the blood pool formed around his feet. The man again cried out as he moaned in pain and turned his face to Chief. In a very weak voice he spoke.

"Gold, there is gold, right here." The man started to stomp his feet and pointed to the floor. Suddenly the prisoner's eyes got really big as his mouth opened and he took his last breath. Cecil's eyes lit up like it was Christmas.

"OK boys, you heard him. Here's the deal, we split the gold 50/50. We get our asses out of this hell hole and no one will be the wiser. Now are you with me?" The room was silent as both Ray and Steve looked at each other. "So what do you two say, boys?" Chief stood there as if nothing had gone wrong, not to mention he had just killed a man that had died right in front of them. Steve and Ray could not believe their ears.

"Are you shitting me? You just tortured that poor guy to death!" shouted Ray as he moved in closer putting his pistol right up to Chief's face. "The hell with the gold and you best keep your hands where I can see them," he shouted a second time at Chief.

Hotel Steve stopped and pondered the situation. No one noticed that the pool of blood was no longer around the dead man's feet. The blood had seeped between the cracks of the cellar door which lay beneath Chief and the dead man. Way down below the blood had to be splattering on a pile of boxes full of gold bars. The man was not lying.

"Now wait a minute, Ray. Let's hear Chief out on this one. We don't want to be too rash. Let's weigh ours options." Chief started feeling pretty good about his odds as a smile formed on his face after he heard the words coming out of Hotel Steve's mouth.

Rain Man quickly looked back at his partner. "Have you lost your mind, Steve? We are here on a mission. Don't do this brother." Suddenly Ray heard Oilcan in his earpiece.

"We're only a few feet down the hall from your location and can see the light coming from the small doorway. We have your coordinates and will be there in two." Ray didn't acknowledge the communication, but he felt better knowing that help was on the way.

In the meantime Skeeter, forever loyal to Chief, was being overlooked as he stood in the corner of the room. Neither Ray nor Steve saw him drop one of his hands down slowly and proceed to slide his weapon out of his holster as he inched his body slowly over in Chief's direction. Ray and Steve were still arguing when Skeeter tossed the gun to Chief, while he quickly jumped and tackled Ray and the two wrestled on the floor. Now armed, Chief shouted "Hold it assholes!" Steve froze as Chief pointed the gun at his head. Ray, being a large man himself, had gained the upper hand on Skeeter as he rolled over on top with his hands around his throat, but both stopped fighting when they heard Chief shout.

"Hold it right there Rain Man or I'll blow a hole in your partner's head." Ray could only look at his partner. There was nothing he could do or say. Skeeter slithered his way out from underneath Ray. Ray remained still, knowing that help was on the way with Oilcan and Recoil only feet away from rescuing them.

"It's OK, Ray, don't worry, this piece of shit ain't going to shoot me." Hotel Steve stood with his arms outstretched as he stared at the barrel of the gun. He then watched as Chief slowly removed the safety and without any thought of remorse he placed the barrel to Steve's head. Even then Steve felt assured this was only a bluff, knowing full well that one of his very own was not about to shoot. He was dead wrong.

Ray screamed out "No!" as Chief pulled the trigger back, and then bam, fired the gun. Steve "Hotel" Hyatt was killed instantly as he was knocked backwards hard against the wall and slid slowly to the basement floor. He was shot with a single bullet, right in his forehead. His blood was splattered all over the other three as Chief started laughing.

"Whoops," said Chief in a soft voice. "Damn, Steve, you made a big old mess," as Chief wiped Steve's blood off his face. He was still laughing.

During this mayhem Recoil eased up alongside Ray as he lay on the floor. Recoil then stood up behind Skeeter and placed his gun to the back of his head. "Don't move," RC whispered in Skeeter's ear. Chief didn't have a clue and was still admiring his marksmanship as he was being surrounded when Oilcan Owens made his own way around the room. He then moved out from the darkness and very carefully and slowly placed his weapon on the back of Chief's neck. He then cocked the hammer back into position.

"Now drop the gun, asshole," Oilcan ordered his once team member, and suddenly Chief looked over to the right and saw that Skeeter was also being held at gunpoint. Without a fight of any kind Chief put his hands in the air. Quickly the two were wrestled down to the ground on their stomachs as electrical zip ties were applied to their wrists. A few minutes later Jack and Rhys made their way down to the cellar as well, but by this time Chief and Skeeter were already under military custody. Jack just shook his head as he saw the two being taken out of the basement. He could not believe this had happened in his outfit as he stared at Steve Hyatt's body lying on the floor.

"Too bad it wasn't you, boss," said Chief as he walked by Jack. Jack and Rhys both turned as if they were going to hit him. Jack could not understand Chief's actions and he had to ask.

"What the hell is wrong with you, Locklear," asked Jack as Chief walked by. "Why Hyatt? What is this all about in the first place? I'm talking to you, ranger!" he shouted.

Chief slowly turned back to face his commander. "He was too greedy, boss; he killed that poor fella sitting in that chair right there," as he pointed to the dead Iraqi soldier. "Man, all he talked about was getting gold; we can't have that in this man's Army! Now can we?"

"That's a damn lie and you know it you crazy son of a bitch. You killed that man, you killed both of them you freaking psycho nut job," shouted Ray as both Wise and Locklear were taken out of the room.

"Get him up," Jack ordered both Ray and Oilcan as they quickly grabbed and carried Steve's lifeless body up the stairs and out of the room.

Jack and Rhys watched as one of their own men was carried off. Rhys turned and looked at his commander. "What now Commander Womack?" asked

Rhys as he waited for instructions and wondered where they stood in the mission.

"What now? The mission, Lieutenant, that's what now. It is still the mission." He then pointed at Chief and Skeeter. "I want those two held somewhere till we finish the mission in finding Hussein. I don't care if you have to hogtie them to a tree. We are going to search this place from top to bottom before we leave, am I understood?"

"Sir, yes sir."

Lieutenant Rhys Garret made sure that Commander Womack's order was carried out. Each man did his part in covering every inch of the 69-room palace, but still there was no sign of the ruler, nor any military presence to be found either. The mission seemed to have been botched from the start.

Suddenly Jack heard the roar of trucks. He looked out the front and saw trucks loaded with Iraqi soldiers heading his way. He watched the caravan as it started to pour across the bridge which led to the entrance of the palace. Along with the troop carriers there were also T-54 fuel tankers making their way toward the palace. Jack wondered why tankers would be with them and noted their movement.

It would be years later when Jack would find out the British Army, in a routine traffic stop, would accidentally stumble onto the answer. And it was gold. Over a million dollars in gold brick was found in those same fuel trucks. Those were the gold bars that Chief and Skeeter were after the whole time.

But now all Jack was thinking was to get out and get out now! So without hesitation the word was given as Jack shouted the order and it was clear to everyone it was time to leave.

"Bug out," was the word given by Jack. Their time was up along with the mission as Jack gathered his men and quickly studied for a way to sneak back over the palace's walls. With Chief and Skeeter in tow and Hotel being carried back by Ray and Rhys, everyone made it back to their cargo truck. Rain Man resumed his position behind the steering wheel but this time without Hotel Steve. He looked at the empty seat to his right, but then the door opened and Commander Jack filled it as Ray started the Deuce and a Half.

The sun was about to rise. Jack knew that in the Muslim faith, Muslims had prayer five times a day, the first of which was called the Fajr. Jack also knew that the first prayer could be prayed anytime between the break of dawn and sunrise, but not during the sun's rising. The trick now was to use this time of prayer to make their way to the airport and out of Baghdad without being detected, and the plan worked.

The palace was only a couple of miles or so from the airport, where their aircraft was on the ready assuming that the men made it that far. Luckily that would be only part of the mission that did go as planned. Without a problem the men made it the plane and climbed aboard. Jack stood beside the doorway to the plane making sure everyone got in with all their gear as he looked back over his shoulder and watched the sun rise to start a new day.

His mind was full of all kinds of thoughts, as he could not help but wonder what the hell went wrong, as he closed the door to the aircraft. Jack climbed in his seat beside the pilot as the plane taxied down the runway. It had been a long night as Jack felt the air pressure as the plane soared up and off the runway and into the morning sky as he and his men finally left Baghdad, marking this mission as over. But this one would go down as a failed mission. He looked back at Hotel Steve's body lying on the deck of the aircraft. This was the only failed mission in his whole career. Jack had lost men before, but this was the only time that Jackson Randall Womack's mission objectives were not achieved.

This failure would be his last mission in a Navy uniform and that's something that Jack would carry with him for the rest of his life. Nor would Jack ever understand the barbaric and treasonous actions of Corporal Cecil "Chief" Locklear, or Specialist Thomas "Skeeter" Wise. Only a special court-martial would have to determine their fate but that too would haunt Jack for years.

The only good news Jack could take out of this was that he was going home to retirement. Only a couple of weeks now and he could not wait to be back in Connie's arms. She was the woman of his dreams and in those arms is where he wanted to be for the rest of his life. A new chapter of their life was about to begin, and Jack Womack could not wait.

Hero's

Welcome

Chapter 7

THE LOCKHEED P-3 ORION TURBOPROP
AIRCRAFT WAS STILL TAXYING down the runway
at Andrews Air Force Base as Connie and Kay
frantically waved, not knowing if Jack was watching
them or not. The large gray Navy submarine hunter and
cargo aircraft slowly made its way closer to the arrival
gate. The 200 or so friends and family members who
were there to greet their loved ones would be divided
into two groups. One group was waiting for their living
loved ones to be coming down the stairs to cheers of joy.
The second group was waiting to greet the bodies of
their loved ones who had made the ultimate sacrifice.

Connie could not stand the wait and was about to explode to see her Jack as the huge aircraft finally came to rest. The large crowd was silent. You could hear the marching feet of the flag-waving color guard who were the first to march out to meet the aircraft. The first door to open was the large cargo bay in the rear of the aircraft where three flag-draped caskets awaited.

In this post-Vietnam War era, the return of the remains of US military personnel was always treated as a solemn occasion and this time was no different. There were no cheers or shouts of joy, only silence from the crowd as they showed their respect as the caskets were slowly lowered out from the back of the plane. One by one each coffin received its own respectful eight pallbearers assigned to carry each casket to one of the three hearses that waited in a row.

In one casket was the body of Steve Eugene Hyatt Jr., aka Hotel Steve. Jack was standing beside the coffin as he and the rest of the military saluted the fallen. Jack proudly escorted his man along with the others to the funeral limousine where they would be driven to their grieving loved ones. Jack and the others slowly marched towards the vehicle with the Navy chaplain in tow as he read scriptures from the book of Matthew from his King James *Bible*. The large back door of the hearse opened as they carefully pushed the coffin into the vehicle, and then the car drove off to the hanger where the grieving families waited. Jack stood silently still saluting long after the car had left.

Connie could not control her tears as she watched her husband dealing with the pain of losing one of his own under his command and all the while wishing he could have done something differently that would have helped save Hotel's life. She could only watch and feel Jack's pain as he finally dropped his arm from his salute and turned towards the crowd in search of Connie, his love. With Connie frantically waving her arms in the air Jack quickly picked her out of the crowd and headed her way as the regular passenger door to the aircraft opened. The second group of passengers appeared to some cheers and shouts of joy, but the crowd was still trying to show some respect for the dead as they greeted their own loved ones with less fanfare than usual.

Kay watched as Connie and Jack devoured each other in a long passionate embrace. Jack covered each inch of her face in kisses followed by a long romantic kiss. It was as if they were all alone with no one within miles of the two lovers. Kay watched patiently as the two finally came up for air and just stood there looking at each other.

"Hey there, babe," Jack shouted, staring at his beautiful wife.

"Hey there yourself, handsome," Connie replied, as they kissed again and Jack gave her another big hug.

Kay finally broke her silence. "Hey Jack, you two need to get a room." Jack looked up with one eye open, in the middle of yet another passionate kiss.

"Hey Kay, I did not know you were here." As the two finally broke off their lip lock, embarrassment caused them to back off of each other as he started to straighten his clothes and she to fix her hair a little.

"Oh Jack, I'm so sorry you lost a man, are you OK sweetheart?" as Connie hugged and kissed him on the cheek and held his hand.

"Let's get to the house babe. I'm ready to go," he said trying to avoid her question. She gave his hand a little squeeze to let him know she understood.

Kay leaned over and gave Jack a welcome home hug and a kiss, then turned and hugged Connie goodbye. "I'm going to run, again welcome home, Jack. Now you two be careful and don't hurt each other," as she laughed. "I need to get back to Georgetown. I'll see you for lunch tomorrow, right Connie?"

"That's right, I'll see you then." She then stopped and looked back at Kay as she opened the car door. "What's in Georgetown?"

"We'll talk about it tomorrow," and again she laughed as she got in her British racing green MG Midget and drove out of the parking lot. The two watched as she left and turned once again to each other and after a quick kiss, they, too, made their way to the parking lot.

Once in the car Jack sat behind the steering wheel, staring out the windshield without saying a word. He had not spoken to Connie as they walked all the way to the car in the parking lot. And she knew something was on his mind.

"Are you going to tell me or not?" she asked, sitting in the passenger seat of their car.

"Twenty years, over 140 successful missions without a problem, every one of which was deemed a success. And on my last operation this happens." He then turned and looked Connie straight in the eye. "Babe, we didn't just lose a man. I had two other men go rogue and mutiny on me. They tortured and murdered one Iraqi soldier and two civilians, one of whom was a young girl who was no older than maybe 14. Plus the whole setup, everything, from the intel to reconnaissance was bad. I'm telling you someone is out to get me. Hell, my team was the one that did half of the reconnaissance. I do not understand how this happened," as he lowered his head in shame.

"Could you be court-martialed, is that what they want?"

"No, I don't think so, hell I'm retiring. I'm out anyway. No, somebody had to know Hussein was not there. Somebody knew more than we did, I can tell you that."

"Maybe they did not want you to capture or kill him. Maybe some kind of deal was made in the last minute before you got there. You said you did the intel recon yourself. So at some time Hussein was there and you knew it."

Jack lifted his head up and looked at his beautiful wife. "Damn, Babe, you are good at this mystery-solving business." He started the car and kissed her one more time, "The hell with the Navy. I'm thinking about starting my own company anyway. Let's go see Tricks. How's that old cat doing anyway?"

"He's doing fine, Jack, just fine," as she smiled, knowing that was their cat's name but also their nickname for making love. The shiny red Corvette convertible pulled out of the parking lot and headed home.

Two New Civilians

Chapter 8

JACK PUSHED HIS CHAIR BACK UNDER THE DESK as the idea came back to him. He finally began to write the mission statement of his new company he had dreamed about for years. *Defend the weak. Protect the innocent. Survive the mission.* That's what he would call his new company, DPS Security. He then finished typing out the words in a large font and hit the printer button on his computer. He printed out the words, then taped the page on the wall of his office and stepped back to admire his work as he glanced at it again for the second time.

He turned and started pulling out folders on men he had fought and served with as he laid the dossiers on his desk. He used his rolodex to cross-reference the names with their phone numbers as he started picking out names of men he knew could do the job as he started looking for employees.

Connie looked in to see how he was doing, periodically checking on him as she had done for the last three days. He had been cooped up in his office and she was starting to worry about him after the so-called retirement party he refused go to. This life of being a civilian was new to the both of them, but it seemed to be a little harder on Jack. Connie knew that when Jack got something on his mind he would drop everything else and see it through. This new life and particularly this adventure of being an entrepreneur were no different.

Connie stuck her head in the office doorway. "Dingdong, anyone home?" she said as Jack sat at his desk deep in thought. "I said hello," to get his attention.

"Oh, I'm sorry Babe, I was just thinking. Oh look, here's the name and the mission statement. What do you think?"

"Nice wording, sweetheart, very nice," as she shook her head in agreement. "But dear, where is the money coming from to start this endeavor?" He didn't answer her question. Instead, he started explaining how he was so tired of still working for the government for the last few years as a contractor but not getting the moneys or recognition a company would receive.

So a company was what he was going to build, and build it in the same manner as the military that he knew so well. The foundation would start with great men and women, all handpicked specialists in their respective field of expertise. Cream of the crop, all former SEALs, Rangers, and Delta Force guys would be the foundation. The administration side would be ex-officers with great military backgrounds, plus business-minded managers and office personnel.

She glanced at him with a smile. She leaned over and kissed him and walked out of the room knowing she was not about to stop his dream. Plus she had a few dreams of her own, and being a new civilian for the last few years was treating Connie fine. She had been working for Jack's friend, Bob Wesson, for several years now and had become his number one insurance investigator. Now, with Lloyd's of London calling her for employment nearly every month, it was getting harder every day to continue working for Bob.

She loved Bob Wesson, her boss, and one of Jack's insurance buddies. Being a woman, without Bob she would have never gotten into the insurance investigation business. Who needs the glamour of a big-name company anyway; it was only Lloyd's, the largest and most prestigious insurance company in the world. God, she wanted to work for them so bad she could taste it, but she would kick herself if Bob, or Jack for that matter, knew she was thinking about it. For right now she would help Jack with his dream and that is what she did.

For weeks she and Jack called old friends, made new ones, sent out letters asking for résumés, asking friends of friends to ask for résumés, and anyone else they knew who could send them résumés or a name. They spent their own money so Jack could fly to meet people who were worth the trip to see in person. They manned the phones talking to others, and slowly but surely the Womacks started building their very own security company made up exclusively of mercenaries— soldiers of fortune some would call them. But like Jack said, they were the best of the best and the finest soldiers he and Connie could find.

Having a great product is one thing. Now they had to sell it, and companies were usually reluctant to go with an unknown. So Connie started calling on some of her insurance clients and businesses she had worked with helping to recover stolen goods and artifacts. Nevertheless, they, too, were slow to come on board.

Then one morning shortly two years after Jack had retired, on February 24th at 9:18 AM came the first World Trade Center bombing. It happened when a truck bomb detonated below the parking deck under the north tower of the WTC in New York City. America got its first taste of a foreign-born terrorist attack. It was not as big a story at the time in comparison to the 9-11 World Trade Center attack.

But a lot of companies started paying close attention to the world events as more business had moved overseas to Muslim counties and felt that they were in harm's way. Whatever the reason, Jack and Connie's new startup started receiving phone calls, and the phones never stopped ringing after that. From Riyadh, Saudi Arabia, to Phuket, Thailand, people needed security and protection and were willing to spend big money for it. Where governments' protection ended Connie and Jack's company began. In just a few years DPS Security was up and running throughout the world.

The last piece of the puzzle was completed once Rhys Garret retired and came on board; the company was no longer a dream, but a well-oiled machine.

Big-League Dreams

Chapter 9

A PILE OF BROCHURES AND LEAFLETS from several insurance companies lay on Connie's desk, as she gave the leaflets a second and third look. She did love working with Bob Wesson and his company, but she had to make up her mind where she was going to work. Was it back to the old or forward with the new? The time for decisions was here and on this day Connie had finally come to a conclusion. She sat there thinking that Lloyd's of London would not continue calling forever and

Jack was set with his own company doing his thing now that DSP Security was doing so well.

No, now was her time, Connie thought, as she picked up the brochure from Lloyd's of London and read it for the 100th time.

Known simply as Lloyd's, it was founded in 1686 as Lloyd's Coffee House by owner and operator Edward Lloyd on Tower Street in London. The coffee shop was a popular place for sailors, merchants, and ship owners, and it quickly became a place to obtain marine insurance.

Connie laid the brochure down on her desk. "That place is over 300 years old, they must be doing something right," she reasoned aloud. She picked up the brochure and her coffee cup at the same time and read over it once more.

Located in London's financial district, Lloyd's is not an insurance company at all. Rather it is a corporate body governed by the Lloyd's Act of 1871 and subsequent acts of Parliament and operates partially as a marketplace with multiple financial backers. These backers are grouped in syndicates and together they pool their money, which helps spread the risk. These underwriters are both corporations and private individuals. The private folks are known in the trade as the Names.

Connie once again laid the piece of paper down but this time she picked up the phone and dialed the number at the bottom of the page. This time she was ready, and the world would soon know who Connie Womack was, and Bob Wesson would just have to understand. Her heart seemed to beat in rhythm with every ring the phone made.

"Lloyd's of London, Wendy speaking, may I help you?" the person on the phone said.

"Yes, Connie Womack calling Linwood Massey please. I'm returning his call." The secretary placed her on hold and soon her new boss was on the other end.

"Hello, Linwood Massey here. How may I help you?" Connie couldn't talk at first. "Hello, is anyone there? This is Linwood Massey with Lloyd's, hello."

Finally Connie spoke up. "Mr. Massey, Connie Womack calling, how are you doing today?"

"Connie, if you're calling for a position with us, I'm doing great!" Connie placed her hand over the phone's mouth piece and held back a scream of delight.

"Yes, Mr. Massey, I am, so the position of investigator is still open?"

"For you it is. Why don't you fly up here to the New York office and we'll make sure it's the right fit for you? What do you say to that, Ms. Womack, easy enough?"

"Sure, when do you want to see me?" she said, drumming her fingers on the desk top.

"I'll have my secretary Wendy call with all the particulars first thing tomorrow. And Connie, don't worry about Bob Wesson. I know him well and he is a good man. He knows this is the right move for you. He's lucky he has kept you this long. You are too good Ms. Womack, and Lloyd's of London will be proud to have you as a part of this company."

"Well thank you, Mr. Massey."

"Please call me Linwood."

"Well OK, Mr. Linwood, I guess I'll see you in a few days, and thank you so much. I will not let you down," she said as she hung up the phone with a smile on her face.

"Damn, you did it girl, you are going to the big leagues!" Connie said out loud. And without warning Tricks the cat jumped up on the desk to celebrate alongside of his master. Connie patted the cat and thoughts ran through her mind. She could not wait to tell Jack but she would have to. Again, he was gone and in some third world nightmare, trying to save a village out in nowhere Africa this time.

But that was their life and for 20 some years it had worked pretty darn well. Nevertheless, she did miss him so, but she knew he would call in a few days. He always did, and she could tell him then. But now she had to go shopping and get ready for the big day in New York, or maybe stay home and curl up with a new book and a nice bottle of wine. That sounded better to her as Tricks kept purring along.

Suddenly the phone rang and Tricks was off and running. Connie answered the phone and it was Bob

Wesson on the other end. "Connie, I need your help. We have a situation down here at the office. I need for you come down here, now! Can you do that, come down now?" She could hear the panic in his voice.

"Now calm down Bob and tell me what it is. What's going on at the office? Has the coffee machine broken or something?"

"No, Connie, there's a body on the floor."

"What?" she shouted after hearing something completely out of the blue.

"There's a dead man lying in my office, Connie. I don't know what to do."

"For God sake, Bob, call the police and I'll be there in 10 minutes. And listen to me Bob, don't touch or move anything. You understand me? And lock the door. I'll be right there."

Connie quickly hung up the phone and dialed Kay's number and waited for her to answer. "Come on; pick up the phone, damn it." She impatiently drummed her fingers on the desk top.

After numerous rings Kay answered. "Kay, I need your help. Bob Wesson is in trouble."

"Connie, I'm having a friend over and well, now is not a good time, sweetheart. I know you must understand the situation, don't you?"

Connie understood her best friend was in the middle of having sex and hated to interrupt, but she really needed her expertise and would not take no as an answer. "Girl I said I need your help! Now get your ass off the couch or out of that damn bed, kiss that boy goodbye, and get your ass over to my office downtown as quick as you can. There's a dead body lying in my freaking office building, OK! Oh, by the way I love you. Thanks."

Kay turned over in bed just in time to see her newfound lover as he walked out of the bedroom wearing nothing but a smile.

"Damn, I hate her sometimes."

Body of

Evidence

Chapter 10

DOZENS OF POLICE CARS WERE SCATTERED LIKE a derailed train, which littered both sides of the street and sidewalks along 10th Street in downtown Washington, DC, in front of Connie's office building. She watched as police and other city officials scurried in and out of the building to which she was headed. It was adjacent to the Boston Mutual Life Insurance offices and just down the street only one block from the Ford's Theatre.

Along with the EMT folks Connie counted several ambulances and of course they threw in a couple of fire trucks for good measure. Wow, leave it up to the DC Metro Police and the other emergency response teams to respond in utter overkill. But of course it always depends on which side of town a crime occurred in, and in this case overkill was in order being it was directly across the street from the J. Edgar Hoover Building. She shook her head in disbelief, yeah, overkill alright she thought as she proceeded across the street.

"Hey, Connie, how's things?"

She walked up to an officer setting a perimeter with yellow tape. "Hello there Pete, mind if I come through?"

"No, no come on in Connie, I'm sure they're all waiting on you," he laughed.

"Yeah, I bet so, especially Detective Baranski."

"I hope you steal his thunder again but be careful. He's a little touchy these days. Wife got smart; she finally left his cheating ass."

"Now Pete, everyone has problems, you take care." She patted him on the shoulder and walked closer to the building.

"Connie Womack, girlfriend. You're looking extra good today. My, my, I must say! Oh how's Jack, is he still out of town?" asked Detective Tommy Riddle. Tommy was a little overweight and a little overbearing, with a large beer belly and red curly hair and a very pale complexion, real white like an albino.

Every time he saw Connie he was relentless. This guy never stopped trying to hit on her, but she knew he was harmless; he was also Matt Baranski's detective partner who was not harmless, and he, too, had a thing for Connie, her skills. Matt was so jealous of Connie's ability to solve crimes, but it was more a back and-forth cat-and-mouse thing they had going on, sort of a love/hate thing. She loved to solve crimes and Matt hated her for it.

"No, Tommy, Jack's in the car and he has a gun, a real big one." He started to laugh but still turned to look to make sure she was really kidding.

"Hey funny lady, Matt's waiting on you, and he's pissed."

"He's pissed?"

"Yes, they're saying your boss is being an asshole. He's locked the door and won't let them see the crime scene without you."

Connie laughed out loud, knowing that was what she had told Bob to do and knowing that would get all over Matt. She knew Matt Baranski hated being upstaged, especially by a woman. Deep down a good guy, Matt had grown up with Jack and through him Connie knew how to touch Matt's buttons to set him off and it wasn't hard for her to do. Matter of fact, she and Jack enjoyed it immensely.

She also knew most of the DC police who were in the investigation division, the good ones and the bad. Connie spent a lot of time downtown trying to help out solving several unsolved crimes. Even when she was in the military, they would call for her input.

So it was like a reunion of sorts, old-home week, as she walked up the long set of steps, which led her up and into the huge Hartwell and Wesson Insurance offices. She stopped and looked up to admire the large mural of a sainted angel with her outstretched arms and rays of light extending from her glowing halo, seeming to welcome visitors from her perch high on the ceiling of the foyer. Connie looked up and said her hellos like she did every time she entered the building; after all, she was the one who recovered the mural in Naples from a bunch of drug dealers. "So beautiful," Connie thought as she heard her name being called out across the gallery corridor. She knew it was Bob so she took her time before responding to his shouting.

"Connie we're in here. Please hurry up, please Connie." Standing in the open hallway was a begging and right pitiful looking Bob Wesson. Connie stopped her upward gaze at the mural of the angel and turned to look at her boss.

"Damn, Bob, I figured you would be in jail by now," she replied as she walked over to the doorway of Bob's offices where he was standing.

"This is no time to be a smartass, Connie. Now get your butt in here," Bob pleaded as he opened the door to the next room, which was his secretary's office.

Without anyone in the room it was small, but now it was packed. There was a group of about 15 people—policemen, detectives, forensics folks and EMTs—all crammed in this small little space and they all were waiting on her. Connie was shocked as she looked at the group wedged in the tiny room. "I wasn't about to let them in till you got here."

"Oh, thank God the great Connie Womack has finally arrived," announced Matt Baranski, the head investigator of the DC Metro Police Department. He was stocky with broad shoulders and thick arms, a gym rat for sure. His hair was a real dark brown, too dark for a man in his 50s. Old Matt was probably a consumer of Grecian Formula, or Just for Men, hair coloring. He stood with his large arms crossed, looking pissed for having to wait.

"OK, she is here, Mr. Wesson. Could you please unlock the damn door now? Connie, he would not let us in. Please tell him to open the damn thing before I arrest him for obstruction and then maybe we can solve a crime here today."

"Sure thing, handsome, by the way nice hair job," she said as she passed him and headed toward her boss. "Hey Bob, what the heck?" She wasn't about to let on that she was the one that told him to keep the door locked till she got there.

Bob fumbled with his keys. "I didn't know what to do so I called the police like you told me, but I wanted you to be the first in. I'm sorry," he shouted as he looked over at Detective Baranski.

"Ok, I'm here, let's take a look." Bob rushed by her and everyone else and placed the newfound key in the doorknob, unlocked his office, and opened the door. Matt and Connie walked in the room at the same time. "After you, detective."

"No, ladies first, I insist."

Connie's eyes combed the room with a quick look-over and sure enough a man's body was lying face down right in front of Bob's desk with his arms stretched out across the floor as if he fell out of the sky. Matt called in forensics and quickly they started taking pictures of everything. Matt looked up at Tommy Riddle. "Hey, Riddle, make sure the forensics guys take photos first, then give me a hand with the body. We need to turn him over."

"Sure thing, Matt."

As they were wrestling with that Connie gave the desk and window more attention as she inspected the whole room, more so than the body. With her notepad in hand she recorded lots of information as the body was turned on its back.

"I know that guy!" Riddle said with surprise. "That's Danny Gambaro. He works across the street in the J. Edgar Hoover Building."

"What? He's FBI?"

"No, he's one of their computers guys, you know, a contractor employee."

Connie looked over. "Hey Einstein, his ID is hanging around his neck. Why don't you read that?"

Riddle grabbed the yellow photo ID badge which was attached to a polyester lanyard and read it out loud. "Daniel Gambaro, Dell Technology Level C, that's him. So what makes a low-grade contract employee walk across the street to this building, walk down the hallway and pick this office so he can die in? That's weird."

"No, what's weird is there is no sign of injury, no bullet holes, knife wounds, nothing," said Matt Baranski as he closely examined the body. Connie gave the body a quick look-over and noticed the pale color of skin and his lips and face appeared to be swollen. She then walked back over to Bob's desk and carefully moved a few papers around looking for anything out of the norm. She turned to look once again at the body.

"You guys watch too many police shows on television. Have you ever heard of a heart attack?" She then turned to Bob "You know this guy, Bob?"

"I know his wife, Kimberly; I believe that's her name."

Everyone in the room quickly looked over at Bob after his statement. Bob then realized what it sounded like. "No, no, not like that! I mean she bought insurance on the guy. Two days ago, in fact!"

"Life insurance? Why would she need to see you, Mr. Wesson?" Detective Baranski asked as he stood up from the body and gave Bob his full attention. "Mr.

Wesson, don't you have insurance agents to do that very thing? Why would she have to see you, the owner of the company?"

"Because it was for $10 million, that's why, smartass. To sign off on something that big, that large of a policy is a little bit over my regular agents' pay grade, detective. Hey look, I'm the one that called you guys. I didn't kill anyone."

"Sorry Mr. Wesson, but I have to ask the questions. Now no one is accusing you of anything right now, but we need to get some more information and a few things straight here. So for all you know the guy just walked in your office, unannounced, looked at you, and fell on the floor dead. Is that right, sir?"

Connie walked over to Bob and grabbed his hand. "Bob sit down." Connie pulled his chair out and around from his desk.

"Connie, I don't know what to do. He is talking like I did something here. I'm telling you I did not!"

"Now, Bob, you don't have to say a thing right now, but to look more innocent to the police here I would suggest you give them something."

Bob's voice quivered, showing he was nervous when he spoke. "Tell them like what? Connie, I didn't do anything."

"Tell them your side of the story, Bob. What did really happen in this office?" Connie walked over and picked up a pitcher of water off the bar and poured Bob a glass. As he took a big swallow his hands were noticeably shaking as the three investigators awaited his statement.

"Like I said, this guy's wife came by and wanted to put this large policy on her husband. I told her he would have to take a medical and physical, plus a background check on the two of them. She didn't seem to have a problem with that. But the next week or so the husband called saying he worked across the street and wanted to come by and talk to me about some concerns he had concerning that policy his wife put out on him. He sounded not worried, but more nervous I would say. So I told him to come by anytime."

Connie was still walking around the room looking for clues. "So he came by yesterday as well as today?"

"No, he didn't show up at all yesterday. He didn't call either."

"Had you started the paperwork on the policy, Bob?" Connie asked.

"Yes, I had. She returned the forms a few days later. Everything was filled out, doctor's physical exam, background check, the works." Bob tried to look at the body and quickly turned his head away. "I have the file right here but I can't just hand it over."

Detective Baranski turned to face Bob and started to say something, then stopped. He walked over to the large picture window with the blinds closed, and then he spoke up. "Do you always close your blinds on such a beautiful day like today, Mr. Wesson?"

"What?"

Tommy Riddle leaned over on the desk. "Sir, your blinds, were the blinds open or closed when Mr. Gambaro first arrived here?"

"Yeah, I guess they were open so I might have closed them. I don't know for sure, why?" as he looked directly at Connie. "Maybe, I guess I closed them because of the sun shining in, or so people could not look in, I don't know, Connie. That's the truth."

"So people could not see the body?" questioned Baranski. "Sir, we are on the third floor. You sure you didn't close the blinds before Mr. Gambaro got here?"

Noise from some kind of commotion began to come from the room next door. It began in the room right beside them and moved to outside of Bob's office. Baranski stopped his interrogation when the door opened and sounds of people arguing flooded the office.

"Lady, you can't go in there. No Lady."

"She told me to come down here, now let go, mean man," shouted Kay as two policemen tried to stop her.

"Please let her go officers. She's a doctor and she is with me." Connie smiled while Kay plowed her way through the doorway, then stopped long enough to straighten her dress and fix her hair a little.

They all turned back to focus on the interrogations. "Look at me, sir," Riddle asked, trying to get Bob's attention. "Please answer the question, Mr. Wesson. Were the blinds closed for a reason or not? "shouted Tommy Riddle.

"Wait one minute; you need to hold on Dick Tracy!" Kay saw all she needed to see before she stopped the questioning. 'That's enough, gentlemen. Mr. Wesson is through with your badgering, no more questions today I'm afraid."

"Wait a minute yourself, lady. What are you, his attorney now?" said Baranski looking over at both Kay and Connie. Connie stepped in front of Kay to referee and shield her from Matt.

"Look Matt, Doctor Shirley here needs to do some mental evaluation tests on Mr. Wesson before this questioning goes any further.

"Mental test my ass! He's going to answer me now or he is going downtown to the station right now in handcuffs."

"Excuse me officer, I don't believe so." Kay interrupted.

"That's detective, to you lady, Detective Matt Baranski, thank you very much and who the hell are you?"

"I'm Kay Shirley, Doctor Kay Shirley, Connie's friend," as she pointed to Connie. "I'm also Mr. Wesson's counselor right now."

"But Connie said you were a doctor."

"That's a good thing about being a double major these days. I do prefer being a psychiatrist, but today I believe I will be using my skills as a legal practitioner. In other words, his lawyer," as she pointed at Bob. "Now Mr. Wesson do not say another word please." Bob shook his head in agreement.

Both Baranski and Riddle were pissed.

Kay brushed her hands together and looked over at the two detectives. "Well, it looks like my work here is done. I'll see you gentlemen at the police station if you are so willing to arrest my client."

"Now hold on lady, we only wanted some answers. We don't want to arrest Mr. Wesson. Hell, we know Bob, he's a straight-up guy," Baranski pleaded.

"Then I'd suggest we all meet again somewhere like your office tomorrow or at least somewhere else where there is not a dead man lying on the floor, if that is alright with you gentlemen," suggested Connie. The two men backed off and turned to look at Connie once again. They never noticed Kay as she looked at the body for a quick examination of her own.

"You are a piece of work, Womack. You know that? You set my ass up so you could be here and investigate this office yourself, didn't you? You two ladies have been snooping in here the whole time in efforts to save your boss's ass. Well, we'll see all of you wonderful people downtown tomorrow at 8 o'clock sharp. You three got that?"

Kay stood up from the body and looked over at Connie and then back at Detective Baranski. "I'm so sorry sir, but without an arrest warrant all you can really do is ask. You can't order us without that piece of paper from a judge. You do understand that, don't you?"

Both Matt and Tommy stood there with a blank look on their faces, and Connie was about to cry, holding back the laugher as she watched this unfold before her eyes, knowing these boys weren't used to being confronted by anybody, much less someone as small and refined as Kay Shirley. Baranski had no choice. "Ladies and Mr. Wesson, I would like to invite you three down to the police station tomorrow morning if that's alright with the counselor here. I'm sure it would look favorable to the court if you come down on your own accord."

"That sounds really nice. Great, we'll see you boys in the morning then. Thank you so much detective," said Kay, but the two detectives didn't move.

"Excuse me ladies," as Baranski pointed to the floor, "we still have a little business to attend to here, like having the forensics folks do a little examining and then removing the body, dusting for prints, you know, police stuff. So if you don't mind could you please get the hell out of here."

Kay and Bob walked out of the room. "That means you too Womack. Get out. Your time is up." And with that all three made their way out.

Initial Deception

Dead Danny The IT Guy

Chapter 11

BOB'S HANDS WERE STILL SHAKING as he tried to drink the cup of coffee Connie had offered him a moment ago. After a few failed attempts, coffee stains showing where they spilled down the front of his shirt, he finally gave up and set the cup back down on one of his subordinate's desk. They were in a maze of cubicles that were in one of the smaller offices down the hall from Bob's. Connie closed the room after she made several agents take an unscheduled break. Meanwhile Baranski and other DC police searched Bob's office, or better still, ransacked Bob Wesson's own office while the body was still sprawled in the middle of the floor.

Connie decided on using this office, which was only feet down the hallway from Bob's, so she could get the information out of Bob as quick as possible while it was still fresh on his mind. She pushed down the play and record buttons at the same time on the cassette player to record his statement.

"OK Bob, as you know I'm recording now. Alright then, let's go back to the beginning." Both Bob's and Kay's eyes followed her as their attention was focused on Connie pacing around the office. "So, you said you were in your office this morning. The door opened and suddenly this guy came in and bam, he fell dead on your floor right in front of you. So what did you do?"

Bob didn't say a word. He only stared at the floor in silence.

"I need your help on this Bob, focus, it's really important that we get our stories straight. If there's any chance that Kay and I can help you, you need to tell us everything. So please, tell us what really happened. Please, we need to know the real story."

Bob looked up at Connie. his face wearing a blank expression. He waited a couple of seconds before he spoke, then slowly the words started to come out. He reached out for the same cup of coffee for the second time and decided against it. Then in a real soft voice the letters came out. "CIA." He stopped again for a few seconds. "That's why I called you first Connie, I was scared, and I didn't know what to do. Hell, I still don't."

Connie stopped her pacing and turned to face Bob. "What about the CIA? Did someone at the CIA call you Bob?"

Bob Wesson stood up and walked around the desk and perched on the corner. "No, they didn't call me, Connie, they hired me." Both Kay and Connie looked at each other as the news came out of Bob's mouth.

"What?" they both asked.

"Yeah, well here's the thing, Danny and I both worked for them. Now don't get me wrong, it was from time to time, it's not like we were James Bond and Matt Helm or anything, but yes, we both were hired and worked freelance for the CIA."

"Danny, you mean the dead guy in your office, holy shit Bob! Are you kidding me?" Connie exclaimed.

Kay turned to Bob. "The CIA? Really?" She stopped and looked around the office, then turned back to Bob. "I have a question, Mr. Wesson. So why didn't you call them in this situation? Why drag Connie and me in all of this?"

Bob waved his arms and placed a finger over his lips as if to say not so loud but had no answer.

"Don't worry about Baranski. He can't hear us Bob," as she grabbed the phone receiver. "Now here's the phone. Call your CIA boss, shoot, call Robert Gates the director himself, surely someone over there can tell you what to do in this matter. Heck, I bet they do it all the time; it's probably in their manual. That way, you can leave Kay and me out of it," as Connie held the phone receiver in her outstretched hand.

Kay suddenly realized she was involved and spoke up. "Kay? Oh hell no, not me, no sir. There's no Kay in this picture. Connie you are the one he called, not me! Connie is right. You better call that CIA boss now, Mr. Wesson, I mean it," she threatened.

"Sorry, I can't do it ladies."

"You can't," as both women scolded him at the same time. "Why not?" Connie questioned. "You work for them, not me."

"I think, well Danny and I both thought, that one of our co-workers who work closer to our superior must have been involved as well. I can't go to him right now. Hell, he might have been the one that got Danny killed. I don't know what to do, but I do know that I don't want to be next."

"Killed over what, a bad insurance policy?" she laughed.

"Danny found information that showed that the FBI was doing an undercover job using a few CIA informants. He believed the FBI was not only spying on the CIA, but he found proof that the CIA may have had several FBI agents killed in the process."

"Killed for what, Bob?"

"Danny and I believed it was a cover-up, dealing with a CIA anti-drug program in Venezuela. The Bureau was looking into a few CIA agents; their thought was that the CIA agents in question were shipping a ton of nearly pure cocaine by way of Venezuela to Colombia and finally sent it into the United States.

"The mission was to infiltrate the Colombian gangs that ship cocaine to the United States, but this operation was intended to win the confidence of the Colombian traffickers. The problem was that the agents not only took the cocaine, but they were also stealing the drug money from the same drug cartels from Central America after all the arrests that were made a couple of years ago."

Bob kept talking. "It's also believed that these CIA agents used a few FBI agents once the drugs were in the states so that when the so-called controlled shipments took place it looked legitimate to the criminal investigators. The shipments then ended with arrests and the confiscation of the drugs that were to be uncontrolled shipments. The catch is no one got caught and none of the drugs, controlled or uncontrolled, was ever seized. We are talking over 3,000 pounds of cocaine, ladies, and it all was bought, sold, delivered and funded by US taxpayers.

"Danny had the hard evidence on several of those CIA agents and I believe that's why he was killed. Ask yourself why CIA ranking officer Michael McLandry has resigned. There are 3,000 pounds, that's a lot of free cocaine someone has floating around out there, and somebody has gotten rich."

Connie and Kay sat there as if they had just read a Tom Clancy novel; they could not believe what they were hearing coming out of Bob's mouth. Both women looked at one another until Connie spoke up. "So, what about the crooked FBI agents that helped? Why doesn't the Agency just arrest them, Bob?"

"They can't Connie, those men are dead. One by one they just accidentally vanished. They're gone. You know like that Deputy White House Counsel guy, Vince Foster a few weeks ago, suicide right, suicide my ass. Danny called me yesterday and told me that he believed he had solid evidence on that case and he knew the names of the agents who were involved and was coming right over to tell me. That was yesterday. That's why I called Connie first, and not the police."

Connie was stunned from what she was hearing as she looked over to Kay for her opinion.

"I wish I could see that body again," Kay said.

"I thought you examined the body already," Connie said.

"Well, I did but I didn't know what I was looking for then. He had a very pale face and that's to be expected, but his lips, throat, and face appeared to be swollen, and Bob here said he had trouble breathing before he collapsed on the floor. It's possible it could be anaphylaxis."

"I thought the same thing," answered Connie, as Bob looked at the girls as if they were talking Greek.

"What the hell is anaphylaxis?" he asked. Connie and Kay both turned in his direction as Connie told him the answer.

"It's the body's being overly sensitive to poisoning because of a previous exposure to the poison, Bob. It's like when you overreact to a bee sting when previous bee stings didn't seem to bother you. But now we can't be sure from what we saw. You would have to have a blood test to prove that."

Kay turned and faced Bob to get his attention. "Look here, Bob, if you are looking to fake an accidental death that's as good as any in my book, and real hard to prove otherwise."

"I knew it, I knew they killed him and there is no way I'm going downtown to that police station, no way. Hell, if they hire an IT geek and an insurance agent, don't you think they have someone on the inside of the DC police department? I need to get the hell out of town for a while, and I need your help. If these people want you dead, trust me, you are as good as gone. You have to hide me somewhere and with Jack's connection, well, I thought maybe you would know what to do."

Connie relaxed back in her chair taking all of that information in without saying a word. She leaned over as she cut off the tape player. No one in the room said a word. All three appeared to be in deep thought.

"I think better when I walk around a little," said Connie as she started her pacing again, walking up and down the length of the small office, all the while thinking as she tipped a pencil to her forehead. Kay and Bob hoped she would work it out like she always did. Back and forth, then she would stop, wait a minute and start back at it, back and forth. This repeated for the longest time. Suddenly she stopped pacing and turned, facing them both. "Jack, I'll call Jack. Have you ever been to Mombasa, Kenya? Mombasa is a beautiful town this time of year."

"Rains a lot," said Kay.

"OK, Bob, I still need to work out a few things but here's the rough draft. I'll contact Jack who is in Somalia. You don't want to be there but the country next door is Kenya, and Jack has an office there. We need to fly you out first thing before tomorrow's meeting with the police. I think we can get you to Kenya with no problem; you do have a passport, don't you?"

Bob shook his head yes. "Kenya? Are you kidding me? I'll be a fugitive from justice when I leave the country."

"No sir," Kay spoke up. "You were never arrested and no one, at least no judge, has ordered you to say in this country. As of right now, as far as I see it, sir, you are free to go anywhere in the world, even Kenya." Bob didn't know what to say as Connie finished telling him his itinerary.

"You need to go by your house and pick up a few things, change of clothes, toothbrush, and of course your wife, and then you'll drive out to the Fairview. It's a small airport out in Bowie, Maryland. Jack's office is there."

"OK, airport. Oh my God, I didn't even think of Nancy. Is she going to flip out or what!" He placed his hands over his eyes.

"Now, now, Bob," said Connie. "What part do you think she will be upset about? Is it the part about a dead man in your office or the part where you work undercover with the CIA, or the part about leaving in a moment's notice and flying off tonight to Africa? She should be able to handle all of that, don't you think?"

Bob Wesson was speechless, as reality was finally registering in his brain. "I can't tell her those things. She would flip out."

Connie placed her hand on his shoulder "I was messing with you Bob. You don't tell her anything about today. Just tell her it's a surprise anniversary trip or something. Hell, I don't care what you tell her. But there will be a time that you will need to tell her the truth, tell her that you work for the CIA, and you have to go undercover. You need to tell her sooner rather than later, Bob. But first I'll call Rhys Garret to meet you guys there at the airport. He can arrange the flight, the hotel, and accommodations.

"That should get you taken care of, but first, you need to write down everything about this CIA job so Kay and I can find out what the heck is going on here." She gave the desk a quick look-over. "Here's some paper and a pen so start writing. I will need names, phone

numbers, and address of places to find these people."
She stopped and looked down at Bob as he began to
write. "And Bob, don't you leave me hanging in the wind
on this thing."

"Connie, I would never do that. I thought you
knew that. And if you feel that way I'll stay here and
face the music."

"Oh shut up and get to writing, I love you too."
She turned to Kay shaking her head. "I've got to talk to
Jack and see what he thinks of this situation. It's so
crazy he won't believe me."

"No, he'll believe you alright. He knows you are
a magnet to nut jobs, but you're right. It does sound
pretty crazy."

Securing
Somalia

Chapter 12

THE WINDS FROM THE HELICOPTER BLADES BLEW a small sandstorm of dust in the air as Jack Womack touched down in one of the poorest countries in the world, Somalia, Africa. The Egyptians call it the ancient land of Punt, where pyramidal structures are found. They also value its trees which produce the aromatic gum resins which makes frankincense and myrrh, like in the Bible.

But every time he visited, including this one, Jack thought of it as more of a shit hole as he climbed down from his UH-60, Black Hawk helicopter. It was the same type of aircraft that was used one year earlier in Mogadishu, the same Mogadishu popularized in the movie, *Black Hawk Down*.

Jack hated the place. After all, it was where several of his special forces brethren and others perished. The Pentagon initially reported five Americans lost their lives but the record, however, was corrected to 18 dead and 73 wounded. Jack took the battle of Mogadishu personally as the task force was made up of mostly Navy SEALs, Army Rangers, and Delta Force soldiers. Jack knew a lot of the men that made up the Joint Special Forces Operation as it was called back then. And most of the personnel he hired for his new company came from that branch of the military.

But now Jack was a civilian, no longer in the Navy and no longer defending his country. No, his job was to protect civilians who were employees of a large telecommunications firm called Tele-Net who had hired his company for security. Security in Somalia was a must. No way would a company risk sending people there without security and Jack's company was state of the art, using the best in communication equipment and manpower that was comprised of a small army under his command. Tight security was the only way it would be possible for companies like Tele-Net to benefit.

Years of civil war had totally destroyed the country. Phones, computers, and television communication systems throughout Somalia were in

118

shambles. The area was still a war zone and security was the number one priority, no question about it. Jack and his team of five men were there to evaluate the improvements from his last visit and were to report on the assessments to the company's board members, after two personnel were killed last month.

Not wanting to be caught in the open they quickly deplaned and swiftly removed their gear from the chopper as the two camouflaged Humvees (High Mobility Multipurpose Wheeled Vehicles) pulled up close to the Black Hawk helicopter. As the vehicles came to a stop a tall, thin young man rapidly jumped out of the vehicle. To Jack he appeared to be about 15 or 16 years old as he approached closer to the group of mercenaries.

"Mr. Womack sir, I'm Ronnie Sawyer. On behalf of Tele-Net I welcome you and your men to the Federal Republic of Somalia, the land of totally nothing but guns and dust," said the company's young communications liaison as he shook Jack's hand. Ronnie was a young man, about 27 or so but a very smart and ambitious executive with thinning blonde hair and thick glasses. He volunteered for the job in hopes it would further his chances of higher and quicker promotion within the company. "How was your trip, sir?"

Jack turned to his radio man, Sydney Rountree, aka Spider. "Spider grab those two bags right there," as Jack pointed them out of several and then turned back around to greet his host. "Hey, Ronnie, trip was good but long. How's the weather here in lovely Mogadishu young man?"

"Today hot and tomorrow damn hot, sir, that's about it sir, again welcome." Spider handed Ronnie the two heavy bags.

"I hope you like your gifts. Be sure every supervisor or manager gets one," Jack ordered with authority. Ronnie opened one of the heavy bags to see nothing but about 50 little white aerosol cans of mace or tear gas. "They're good for 20 feet. It will help keep the bad guys at bay until help arrives."

"Thank you, sir, I guess," as he closed up the bags and placed them in the vehicle. "Sir, we are ready if you and your men are." Jack looked to see Spider and the rest of his men standing by with bags in their hands set to go.

"We're good, Mr. Sawyer, ready to go when you are." The six men, plus Ronnie, got into one of the two Humvees, Jack rode with Ronnie as they headed out beyond the gates and the barbwire fencing that surrounded the small private airport and its compound. Out across the vast open desert of Somalia, they headed west toward the company's headquarters. For miles all they saw was windblown sand and rocks and once in a while a dead tree or two. Then they started to see more signs of civil war and tribal conflict. Burned-out villages dotted the landscape, and very little signs of life were anywhere as a very thin dog barked at the convoy. This scenario repeated itself for the duration of the trip as they wound through village after village with nothing to see but devastation.

Suddenly Ronnie remembered the message from the states to Jack. "Oh Sir, I almost forgot that I have a message for you." Ronnie handed him a piece of paper folded into a small square. Jack unfolded the paper and read the short message: To my Love, miss you. Need you to call when you have the time. Thinking of sending two packages to Kenya.

"Ronnie, how much farther is it to headquarters? I need to make a call," Jack asked.

"Not far, sir, about 20 more minutes, that's all, but we have no signal out here sir. I'm afraid you'll have to wait till we get there."

Jack looked over at Spider without saying a word; Spider went straight to work as he grabbed his gear and pulled out a radio phone. It looked very much like a walkie-talkie. He then dialed in the coordinates and quickly handed Jack the phone. Ronnie looked surprised as Jack called Rhys, who was in the office at the Fairview airport.

"Cracker Jack to Captain Crunch, come in Captain Crunch." The phone was full of static but with a twist of a knob it cleared up. After two or three more attempts the phone received a good transmission.

"Roger that, Cracker Jack, how goes it, over," answered Rhys Garret on the other end.

"Just arrived, everything's good here, just checking on messages. How's my little cookie cutter, over?" He was speaking of Connie.

"She's fine, Jack, but needs to talk when you get to a landline, not on open airwaves, but she's fine, no problems, over."

"Roger that, will call her in about 20. Please notify her, over."

Roger that, will notify, Captain Crunch over and out."

Jack handed the phone back to Spider as he pondered what would be so important that she would need his attention now. After all, he just left her a few hours ago but his thoughts of her were abruptly interrupted as the noises of the city streets surrounded him as the convoy entered one of the oldest cities in all of Africa.

The streets of Mogadishu were packed with all kinds of vehicles from cars, jeeps, trucks, even donkey carts filling the dusty streets. If it could move at one time or another it was on the streets of Somalia's capital city. Mogadishu was known locally as Hamar, which supported over two and a half million people and most of them were watching as the caravan moved around the city.

The two Humvees got a lot of attention as people stared while they slowly made their way through the ancient town. Military vehicles were very common in Mogadishu, but what made these so different was because these were in great shape. These vehicles looked brand-new, not the usual beat-up and broken-down dirty trucks with tribal warlord insignia all over them. No, these looked more like brand-new shiny race cars with the Tele-Net logos plastered all over, resembling something like NASCAR vehicles more than military light trucks.

Then, as different as day and night, the vehicles turned left on a new road and a new town appeared. Like the trucks it was all brand-new everything. The men felt as if they were entering the city of OZ, not emerald but still bright and shiny new, new buildings, new streets, curbing, sidewalks and real streets and stoplights that worked. In all it was a new town and right in the middle of it all was the new Tele-Net building.

The Humvees pulled right up to a large gate where concrete barricades sat on either side of the perimeter. The guards walked out to check with the drivers as two men swept mirrors and bomb detection devices underneath the vehicles before they were allowed entry. Once clear of that and they had passed inspection they were instructed to drive thru a very narrow one-lane path and stop in the middle, similar to going through a car wash. Several guards checked everyone's paperwork and passports. After that they advanced a few feet to another checkpoint. This time everyone was to get out of the trucks and was personally searched. Jack liked what he saw as he stepped out of the vehicle and was greeted by one of his employees.

"Ray, everything looks pretty good. I like the new concrete walls, but I want a few more forming more of a zigzag pattern so they don't just run straight through. Other than that, how's the world been treating you this day?"

"Mr. Womack, I mean Jack, everything is fine sir, we are truly living the dream, sir, in this little slice of heaven and you know me I wouldn't want it any other way," he said with a smile.

"Yeah, I know Ray, but at least the pay is good, right," said Jack as they both laughed. Ray Ketchum was as tough as they come, once a professional heavyweight boxer turned US Army Ranger. For years he had worked in unison with Jack's SEAL Team 4 on several covert campaigns. He was hard as nails and strong as a bull and dependable, very dependable. He was on the short list as one of the first men Jack hired.

"Sir, we'll get you and your men's gear but first let's get you out of the heat."

"Sounds good to me, Ray," answered Jack as the men were escorted out of the parking area through a combination of sliding doors as they arrived inside the command center. Ronnie stopped before going through the doorway. He stood still, watching a man riding in a donkey cart as he entered the outer perimeter check point. "That's not right," he thought. The warning alarms suddenly sounded along with the sliding doors quickly shutting when the cart did not stop when told to do so. The men monitoring the TVs saw the cart being pulled by a donkey. The guards shouted halt several times and the cart kept advancing into the compound. Others ran to their stations, armed and loaded. A barricade was moved in front of the advancing cart.

"Ray, sir you need to see this," said a new recruit who was working the controls of the front gate, as he nervously called his superior to check the perimeter breach. The control panel was now lit up like a Christmas tree. "Sir there are more sensors detecting a bomb in the cart sir."

Ray Ketchum without hesitation quickly hit the button on the console as he shouted "Bomb!" causing the perimeter team to open fire on the cart. The Somali who was sitting in the cart knew his fate was sealed as his eyes got wider just before the blast. The explosion sent dust, rock, and body parts flying as the blast rang out.

After the dust had settled Jack and his men looked out the windows to see the carnage but there was nothing left of the man or donkey, just a big red stain on the pavement and blood dripping off the bulletproof glass and concrete walls. The man and donkey were totally disintegrated. The men rushed out to determine what work needed to be done as they inspected the area and checked the perimeter for another breach of any kind.

Ronnie Sawyer was shaking, white as a ghost. He had been caught outside during the lockdown. Before the blast Jack and his men had walked through several of the combination sliding doors but Ronnie's hesitation when he first saw the cart left him outside. Jack and the rest of his men watched and saw that Ronnie was OK as they looked through a two-way mirror window. He was still holding his ears and scared out of his wits. He then furiously started beating on the glass door with his fists. "Hey, open this damn thing."

Ray pushed another button on the control panel, a microphone. Ray's calm voice came out of the outside speakers. "Mr. Sawyer, I'm glad to see that you appear to be alright, but sir please stop and step back so I can let you in."

Ronnie stopped screaming as the door finally opened. He walked in and immediately saw several guys laughing. "Well thanks a lot you meat-headed army dicks," Ronnie said aloud, thinking those guys did it on purpose. Ronnie not being ex-military they were always messing with him, but this time it was for real. Ronnie was still pissed but glad to be alive. As embarrassment started to kick in he, too, started to laugh a little at himself.

Cheers rang out as Ronnie made his way up to the control room. "Thanks a lot, Ray. That was really funny," said Ronnie.

"Sorry sir, but you need to move a little faster when those alarms go off like that, sir." Jack put his arm around the kid as he too was laughing a little.

"It's OK, Ronnie, it's funny now because you were not hurt, but you need to get the doc to check you out and after that how's about you showing us the rest of that company tour."

"Yes sir, will do."

"Now I need to use a phone and call Connie ASAP. And don't let those jarheads give you any more shit, alright?" as Jack gave the kid a pat on the back, thanking God he was OK. *Just a regular old day in Somalia*, Jack thought, now where's that phone?

Suggested Instructions

Chapter 13

CONNIE DUSTED OFF THE LINT FROM THE lampshade and straightened out the wrinkles on the comforter as she waited on the bed beside the phone. The time seemed to move more slowly on a watched clock, her mother always said, so she turned it over on its face and stood up. She started pacing the floor and again, for the hundredth time, she looked at the clock on the nightstand. Knowing she could not see the face of the clock, she walked towards it as the phone suddenly rang. The noise scared her so much she let out a short scream as she placed her hands over her mouth to stop her laugh. She waited a second or two to catch her breath, smoothing out the wrinkles in her dress and fixing her hair a little bit, and then quickly grabbed the receiver.

"Hello?"

"Sweetheart, it's Jack. Are you alright? Rhys said for me to call you."

"Oh Jack, it's great to hear your voice; I miss you so much already. No, I am fine. Dear, the problem is our friend and my boss Bob. I'm afraid he is in a world of trouble. I was thinking maybe he needs to leave the country and go somewhere like Kenya till things here cool down. Somehow Bob got himself involved with the CIA."

"The CIA, are you kidding me?"

"No, and to make matters worse one of his undercover co-workers said he had some dirt on the CIA. Well, he goes missing one day and then the next day he shows up dead in Bob's office. He fell dead on the floor right in front of Bob. Well, Bob flipped out of course and he called me."

"Co-worker, who's this guy?"

"His name is Danny Gambaro. As far as I know he was working in the FBI building as a contract IT computer guy, nobody special that I know of. But the cops, you know Baranski and his gang, came and questioned old Bob; he got all scared and clammed up. He refused to tell the detectives what they want so we are supposed to meet them at the police station tomorrow morning."

"No, he does, not you Connie!"

"Well, you see here's the thing. Bob agreed to the meeting but when we left the room that's when he got Kay and me involved."

"You two involved how?"

"He told us the story that he worked for the CIA and that this dead guy was coming over to tell Bob what he had on the CIA. It was something about drug cartels and, oh get this, the US was buying cocaine from the Venezuelans and giving it to the Colombian drug cartels to infiltrate their drug business. The catch was they were keeping the drugs and the money, pretty crazy right."

Jack didn't say a word, knowing personally the story was true.

"My first thought was to get Bob out of town and ship his ass out of the country. You think Kenya is a safe place?"

"Here's the way I see it. OK, first of all Kay is not involved per se because she is a lawyer, his lawyer. And second, if he leaves the country going through our company it looks like we are colluding. It might not stick in a court of law, but still. So how does this sound? Why don't you call Sam and have him do some checking?"

"Are you talking about Sam Hornaday? I don't know if he still works. Wasn't he real sick a few years back with cancer or something?"

"No, he's fine now and he'll do it for us. Sam's a little older and slower but still a good man. He might jump at the chance to do something. And see what kind of information he can come up with on this other fellow, the dead guy in the office. In the meantime put Bob on ice in the Baltimore safe house and you check out his side of the story. You never know what you might dig up on old Bob."

"That sounds pretty good sweetheart. I knew you would know best how to handle this."

"Now we still can keep the Kenya deal or somewhere else as a possibility, but I put my money on Sam Hornaday. Sam can shine some more light on this CIA, FBI thing. Plus it's cheaper for us. We both love Bob, but sticking him in Baltimore is a lot cheaper vs flying him and his wife halfway across the globe. Now that's just me, what do you think, Babe, it's your ballgame? But whatever you do, be sure you get Rhys to help you. I want you to be safe, OK?"

"I'll be all right, sweetheart, but I'll call Rhys. I guess you're right, Jack. I was going too fast. I'll call Sam when we hang up. Again you are right , we just need some more information on this whole thing." She then changed the subject. "How's Somalia and how's the company building? Please tell the fellows I said hey."

"I'll tell them and look, everything is fine here in good old hot as heck Somalia. Ray Ketchum, you remember him, don't you?"

"I sure do, big man, Ray the boxer, right!"

"Yeah, well, he is doing a great job here with security, looks a lot better than the last time I was here. If everything goes as well as I have seen so far, I should be home in a few days. I'm hoping it won't take too long, at least I don't think it will, but you know how these things go."

"Yeah, I know alright," she said with a hint of sarcasm. "Well you take care and I love you. Please be safe, and I'll stick Bob on ice in Baltimore."

"Sounds good, babe, I love you, take care sweetheart."

"I will Jack, love you too," she said, as she heard the line go dead. She stared at the phone a couple of seconds before she hung it up. And like that she was by herself again in the home beside the bay smelling the fresh sea air, but alone nevertheless. She thought of Jack's suggestion, figuring out the parts she liked and the ones she didn't. Jack knew Connie was her own person and there's no way she was going to do something just because he said so and he was right again. She picked the phone receiver back up and called the airport as Rhys answered.

"I talked to Jack a few minutes ago, Rhys. I need you to meet me in the morning. We are going to Baltimore, but first I need you to make out a dummy flight manifest."

"Where am I going, Connie?"

"You are not going anywhere, and neither are your two passengers."

132

"What?"

"It's been a long day. We'll talk about it in the morning."

Sam's Soul Revival

Chapter 14

THE TELEVISION SCREEN WAS FULL OF SNOW AND STATIC, with the rabbit-ear antenna lying on the floor beside empty beer bottles. The local station signal had been off the air for hours. Stretched out on his dirty blue Lay-z-Boy recliner dead asleep was the once great Sam Hornaday, a retired newspaper reporter for the *Washington Post*. He had grown to hate the political bias of the Washington, DC, elite, and the newspaper business in general. Sam later used those same informants he had used as a reporter to become a private investigator who not only wrote about DC crimes but got paid to solve them.

Sam was a former Vietnam War correspondent and became pretty famous back in the day of the Watergate investigation with the Nixon administration. After all, it was Sam's story which broke the news that scotch tape was left on the doors, causing them not to lock, proving that someone had broken into the rooms of the Democrat headquarters in the Watergate Hotel. That was the one piece of evidence which led to President Nixon's resignation.

For years afterwards Sam was a fixture on the inside dirty little world of Washington's politics and crime, always in the background, knowing the ends and outs to get a good story. But those were years ago when Sam was a young man climbing the corporate ladder, hungry and full of life, trying to right the wrongs and make a name for himself as well. Now, years later, Sam was a broken older man with all of that behind him.

His life now consisted of empty beer and liquor bottles, along with cigar butts littering the floor of his cramped little apartment. Time left on this planet seemed to be more like the enemy to Sam that limited his ability to just enjoy what was left of his so-called golden years. According to Sam Hornaday, his life was over, as days after days were filled by complete and utter boredom.

His doctor's office had finally quit calling to give him information on more lab results that he didn't want to hear. For the last few months he had decided he was through with all the hospitals, all the doctors. Enough with the dreaded chemo and radiation treatments, and he was tired of throwing up all morning and staying awake with hot flashes all night. No, to Sam he had run his race, and in his mind if the rest of his life was going to be a repeat of yesterday, like hundreds of the days before, then Sam Hornaday was hoping that he would not be long for this world. As he slept in his dirty old recliner, he dreamed he would not awaken this time.

Then unexpectedly the phone rang and kept ringing, breaking the silence of Sam's slumber. After the repeated ringing Sam regrettably opened his eyes, then blinked a couple of times to focus on the snowy TV screen. He reached over and grabbed a bottle of Old Crow whiskey to wash out the bad taste in his month. The only reason he was about to answer the loud telephone was to make the damn thing stop ringing.

"Damn, I'm still here," he said to himself as he placed the phone receiver to his ear. "Alright already, I'm coming, hold on." His dry and scratchy throat slowly answered. "Yes hello, this better be someone I want to talk to. Who is it, hello?"

"Hello Sam, Mr. Hornaday, it's Connie. How are you doing this beautiful day?"

"Who, hold on," as he coughed a few times into the phone to clear his throat. "Sorry, who is this again?"

"Mr. Hornaday, it's Connie Womack, Jack's wife, you remember me from our wedding a few years ago, don't you?"

Sam sat up in the chair as he pulled the handle to the recliner and the leg rest pulled in causing him to sit up straight. He wiped the sleep out of his eyes and tried to comprehend what was being said. A few seconds went by before he spoke. "Womack, Commander Jack Womack. Jack, yeah, I remember him, he played middle linebacker for Navy, had six tackles in one game against Notre Dame, yeah, I remember you two getting married. You were a pretty little thing. I don't forget a good brand of whiskey, nor a beautiful lady. Yes, what can I do for you Mrs. Womack?"

"Please call me Connie, Mr. Hornaday."

"And likewise, you can call me Sam. OK, now we got that out of the way, what is it Connie? I don't have all day."

"Sam, Jack and I have a friend, a Mr. Wesson. He owns an insurance company here in town."

"Yes, I know of Bob Wesson. He's a pretty powerful man. What about old Bob?"

Connie then told him the whole story about the CIA and the FBI drug cover-up, the dead man in Bob's office, the whole crazy thing.

"Well, it sounds like Bob is in some shit, but why are you calling me? I don't even know the man other than what I read in the papers, Connie."

"Sir, I want to hire you to do some investigating for us. Jack says you know this town better than anyone."

"Work, hell young lady I haven't worked in years. Shit, I'm about as retired as it gets around here, plus I've got things to do, places to go. Hell, I'm through working, I'm done."

Connie realized that when she first called he had been asleep and it was two o'clock in the afternoon. She had heard that he was sick and had turned into some kind of hermit, probably feeling sorry for himself. "Well, sure if you are that busy I understand, but if you are just too old and can't do the job—I'm so sorry I called. I did not mean to interrupt your daily schedule of important activities. Again, I'm sorry to have bothered you sir."

"Now you just wait one damn minute, little lady. Where do you come off calling me up and insulting my ass by calling me too damn old? I was a war correspondent in both Korea and Nam and after all these years there still isn't an investigator in this town that's got more shit on more people than I do. Hell, lady, J. Edgar himself used to call me trying to find dope on people, so don't you think my ass can't still do a stellar job if I need to. Don't you think I can't for a minute."

"Now, now, Mr. Hornaday, I'm sorry if I offended you. I was not trying to insult you, sir. I'm sure you can do the job. That's why I called you in the first place. Your experience is what I need, and Bob Wesson needs your help now. I was hoping that you could be a part of our team and that would help us both, that's all. Please except my apology, Mr. Hornaday?" she asked. The phone was silent for only a few seconds then he spoke.

"I said to call me Sam. Now when and where do you want to meet so we can discuss this proposition? I don't have all the time in the world you know, like you said, I'm old."

"How is tonight about seven at Morton's Steakhouse downtown, my treat. What do you say, Sam?"

"It's a date, and not to sound like a pervert but for this old man could you please wear something real nice, maybe off the shoulders, Connie? I haven't seen a pretty lady in a long time, maybe something in black."

"You got it Sam, black it shall be. See you there at seven."

Sam sat with a slight smile on his face. It felt a little funny at first, the feeling of being needed. He turned on the lamp beside his chair so he could see more clearly as he slowly stood up from the recliner. With his arms out searching for balance he took his first step. The floor was full of empty beer bottles as he fought his way across the cold wooden floor like a destroyer maneuvering around floating mines.

It took him several minutes of maneuvering, but Sam finally made it to the bathroom. Reality came in with a crushing blow as he stared in the mirror at his own reflection—an ancient relic that once was the top investigator in Washington, DC. *Damn boy, we have a lot of work to do to get you back in shape,* he thought, and started brushing his teeth for starters, knowing the dirty yellow beard was next. It had been a long time since someone asked Sam Hornaday for help on a case. He was as excited as a school boy. He held the straight razor with both hands hoping not to cut himself. After all, he had a date with a pretty lady tonight. And tonight the real Sam Hornaday was going to show up.

He stopped and stared at his reflection and spoke to himself again. "Well Sam, I hope we're getting in this game in time to help us both. I only wonder what in the world has old Bob gotten us into this time."

Bob's Safehouse Retreat

Chapter 15

CONNIE HUNG UP THE PHONE KNOWING she needed to make one more call. There was no way she could make it to her interview in New York with Lloyd's of London next week, not with everything going on with Bob. That would be too much, no way. She pulled her rolodex across her desk top. Her fingers danced through the index cards on the small rotating spindle till she reached the L's. Are you sure, she thought again? Her hands were shaking as she went ahead and called and listened to the phone ring.

"Yes, thank you for calling the east coast office of Lloyd's of London Insurance Company. This is Mr. Massey's office, may I help you?"

"Wendy, Connie Womack. I'm supposed to meet with Mr. Massey next week."

"Yes Connie, I was going to call you earlier. I have your new employee papers ready to go plus your airplane tickets. I'm going to mail them overnight to your house. Mr. Massey is so excited. Everyone here is looking forward to meeting you. Do you a have any questions for me?"

Connie wanted this job so badly; she thought for a second then answered. "No, I'm fine, I was just checking."

"Alright then, I'll see you next week, looking forward to it."

"Likewise," Connie replied and hung up the phone. *Well, way to go Womack. You couldn't tell her that you would not be able to come next week because of everything going on. I see you don't have your big girl panties on today.* The phone then rang making her jump a little, as she caught her breath and answered hello.

"Connie, this is Bob. What's going on with your man Mr. Garret? Nancy and I are here at the airport and now he is saying the trip is off. So what I'm supposed to do now?"

"Don't worry Bob, everything is fine. Tell Mr. Garret that I'll be there in a few minutes to pick you and your wife up."

"OK, I was worried something bad had happened."

"No, it's all good Bob. I'll see you in a few." She hung up the phone and headed out the door. *And I have to meet with Mr. Hornaday tonight, man what a day so far.* She grabbed her pocketbook and car keys and out the door she went.

The skies finally started to clear, and the rain stopped about the same time that the black SUV pulled up in front of one of many old warehouses. The street block was full of them. The street was also known for the old-style row houses, but by now all but a few had been torn down one by one over the years and now there was little left but empty lots and warehouses.

Rhys looked down the empty street near the corner of Sterrett Street and West Hamburg Street in downtown Baltimore, his hometown and near where he was raised, much like his hero Babe Ruth, who was also an orphan. This was once a throbbing neighborhood and only a few blocks from Babe Ruth's birthplace. He and his buddies would play in the streets not too far from the Oriole Park where the Baltimore Orioles baseball team played now, but still a few miles from where the old War Memorial Stadium stood. Rhys tried to go to every game at that old stadium, which was built back in the 1920s when the Babe himself played ball. Its location was 900 East 33rd Street, now renamed Babe

Ruth Plaza. Rhys turned to help Bob and his wife Nancy, a small but round lady with a pretty smile, get out of the large Suburban SUV.

"Well folks, we're here. Watch your head, Mrs. Wesson. Don't be scared, it gets better on the inside, Mrs. Wesson. Bob watch your step," as they disembarked the vehicle. Connie was still sitting in the passenger's seat reading a Lloyd's of London brochure when Rhys pounded the side of the door with his fist to get her attention. She looked up. "Now if everyone will follow me," he said looking directly at Connie. She finally got out of the car.

The old red brick warehouse was about the only thing still standing on the block and there were no pedestrians. Once Rhys got everyone out of the vehicle he quickly herded everyone down a small alleyway in an attempt not to be seen. He didn't want anyone questioning why they were there. His directions led all four to a large rusted metal door with a huge keypad lock on it. Surveillance cameras dotted the area but were out of plain sight to any passerby. As Rhys typed out the combination they could hear the bolts as they were thrown back and the door opened with ease.

"Please hurry, step inside," he instructed as the rest scurried into the doorway which led them straight to another door, only feet away from each other. This time the door looked very modern and was made of stainless steel. Rhys used a finger scanner as he pressed his thumb on the red laser light causing the small red light to move across his fingerprint as it scanned for a match in the company's personnel database for the right information.

Once the process was completed the door opened with very little effort. "OK, folks make yourselves at home. You're going to be here a while." Nancy's and Bob's mouths opened wide as they stood and looked around the apartment. It looked like something you would see on TV of the rich and famous. It was very modern and very large, with huge ceilings about 20 feet high and everything was all white. The place was clean as a pen but there were no doors anywhere. The place looked like an open-air loft with one huge room downstairs, kitchen, and living room with bar, and upstairs were the three bedrooms and again no doors, even to the bathroom.

"What's with the doors or the lack of them, Rhys?" asked Bob as he questioned the architecture.

"Security, better for us to see you, and for you to see the bad guys, Bob. Plus it makes it easier to see someone sneaking around the apartment."

"Yeah, but wouldn't they be able to see me as well?"

"Yes sir, but you would definitely know by then that someone was inside."

"I'm afraid I don't understand."

Then Connie spoke up. "You see, Bob, you will be monitored at all times, both you and Nancy. We will inform you if we see something out of the ordinary. And you two will have the ability to monitor movement from outside as well. Come look at this." Connie walked over to a large TV screen and pressed a button. The surveillance cameras captured all 10 different pictures on 10 smaller screen views from 10 different angles and places.

"You will be able to monitor in real time and record to be played back if needed." She then pointed to both Rhys and herself. "We will be able to see the same footage inside and out of the apartment in a three-block perimeter."

"Inside there are no doors, and why is every damn thing white? Answer me that one and how about some privacy around here for us?" asked Bob, as Nancy walked over and gave him a hug, feeling a little insecure and very vulnerable.

"Here Nancy, you touch this button and there's one just like it upstairs in your bedroom. If you ever need more privacy you press that button, the yellow one. Now it is on a timer and that's for safety. And all this information is in this book, including the info on the saferoom upstairs off the bedroom. If you have to use it the doors will lock and stay locked for 12 hours. It's all in here," as Connie held the white book in the air.

"As far as everything being white, well that will make other objects stand out on the monitors and be easier for us see something or someone better against the background of white, that's all."

"Damn, Connie, Jack's got a hell of a setup here. Have you ever used it before?"

"Just once," said Rhys, and that's all he would say about that. Connie quickly turned to look over at Rhys. She was surprised at his answer. "OK then, I'll go outside and get your things. Connie can finish up by showing you guys the rest of the house like the library and the kitchen while I'm doing that. Is everybody OK with that then?" Both Bob and Nancy shook their heads in the affirmative. Rhys walked out the door. They could hear the door as it locked behind him.

"Damn, Connie you do live in a James Bond world. I had no idea this kind of place even existed." Both he and Nancy sat down on the white sofa and looked up to her for an answer, and there was not one.

Connie went on to point in the direction of the kitchen. "The freezer and refrigerator are both full of food." She walked over to the pantry and pointed. "The pantry is over here and stocked with dry goods, flour, cornmeal cereal, coffee, even dried beans. But most of the food is freeze-dried, frozen or canned for longer shelf life. Any questions before I leave, Bob, Nancy? And again read the white notebook. That will help a lot.

"In the meantime the phone, it's right here," as she pulled open a kitchen drawer. "It will call only Rhys and no one else so remember, if anyone shows up other than Rhys, you need to use this phone." Bob and Nancy looked in the drawer as if they were going to see a snake.

"Here's your gun if you think you need it. She's loaded and ready to go. Again it's right here in this drawer," she said as she shut the second drawer. "Now remember you guys are not prisoners, it's for your own safety, and by the way the windows are painted to look like windows, but they are not, so it is day time all the time in here." Suddenly a green light flashed, and the door opened as Rhys dropped their luggage on the floor and looked at Connie. She walked over to the door when she saw Rhys.

"You ready, Connie? We need to go now."

"Sure, hold on a second. Now Bob, Kay will be at the police station in the morning on your behalf. Is there anything I need to tell her before she goes that you can think of?"

"No, I can't think of anything. To tell you the truth right now, Connie, I can't think of anything at all. This whole thing is pretty overwhelming to say the least."

"I understand, Bob, but I need for you two to hang in there. This will be over soon. I'm meeting a gentleman tonight who is going to help. I truly believe he can and he will. Now remember what I said, and read the book," as she leaned over and hugged Nancy and kissed Bob on the cheek good bye. The Wessons both waved as the stainless-steel door shut and locked.

Bob started looking around the room. "Now where's that damn book?" he asked.

Food For Thought

Chapter 16

THE STREETS OF WASHINGTON WERE STILL WET, even though the rain had finally stopped. Connie looked out the window of the restaurant with concern that her guest was going to be a no-show; after all, it was close to eight o'clock. He was only one hour late, that's all, she kept telling herself as she raised her hand to attract the waiter's attention.

"Yes ma'am, would you like another glass of wine or maybe some more water at this point?"

"No, that will be all I'm afraid, just the check please. It looks as if my friend is not coming."

"Yes ma'am, I'll be right back."

Tired of sitting for over an hour, Connie stood up to stretch her legs. At that point she could see over the rest of the patrons who were eating, and she then noticed a man who was standing in the doorway entrance of Morton's who appeared to be Sam. She quickly raised her hand and began to wave it to get his attention. He saw her and waved back as he moved across the floor in her direction. The closer he got to her it became apparent it was indeed Sam, but he was soaking wet, standing in front of her still dripping large puddles of water on the black and white tile floor.

"Oh my God, Sam, you are soaked to the skin," as she motioned to the waiter for his attention. "Sam, I'm so sorry. Waiter please bring some towels, lots of them please."

"Yes, absolutely ma'am."

"Sorry I'm late. I don't have a car and well, I needed to walk some but I got caught in the rain." In reality he had got cold feet and got rained on in the park when he was wondering if he should make the meeting with Connie in the first place. "That damn weather man was off a bit. I should have gotten a cab," he said as the waiter came over carrying a few towels.

"Bless your heart," said Connie as the waiter handed Sam the towels.

"Please sir, you can go in the restroom if you like and Henry can help you clean up a bit."

"Thank you, young man, sounds like a good idea. I'll be right back, Connie," as Sam took the towels and headed to the restroom. Inside stood a distinguished looking restroom attendant with his setup of hand lotions, mouth washes, several fragrances of men's cologne and breath mints all laid out on the counter top beside the sink and his tip jar. He noticed the old man when he came in still dripping from being soaking wet.

"Sir, let me help you. What size shirt do you wear?"

"What size shirt, you guys selling shirts too? Damn I thought this was a bathroom not Macy's department store."

"No, I'm sorry sir. I'm just trying to help. I'm not trying to sell you anything. For emergencies I keep a few dress shirts on hand," as he pulled out a white shirt and handed it to Sam. "Here you go sir, one fresh, dry-cleaned, white oxford cloth, button-down shirt, by Arrow. It's 16½ neck, 34 long, how's that look?"

"Great and that's my size," said Sam as he started to change into his new shirt.

"Hand me those trousers. I can dry them off with this hair dryer while you change into your shirt and here's a comb and some hair gel. We've got to get you looking right tonight sir."

"Henry, you are something else. I thank you so much."

"It's my pleasure sir, my pleasure."

A few minutes later Sam came out from the restroom a different looking man. Connie stood up as her mouth literally dropped open. She could not believe her eyes when Sam walked back to the table.

"Excuse me, madam, is it alright if I have a seat at your table? Sorry to make you wait so long."

"My God, Sam, you look great! Who's working in that bathroom, Vidal Sassoon?"

He laughed a little. "No, I believe his name is Henry, nice man that Henry," said Sam as he helped Connie back to her seat and the two sat down. "So what's so important? Do you really think getting an old man like me out of mothballs is going to help this Wesson fellow?"

The waiter came back around to the table. "Waiter please, we would both like a glass of chardonnay."

"No wine for me, dear. I think tonight I'll just have a coke." Connie realized Sam had a drinking problem in the past and changed her order as well.

"Sure, that sounds good to me as well, make that two Cokes. I'll take a diet."

"Hell, I can't stop doing everything bad so make mine a high-test, regular Coke for me, please," he said and they both laughed.

"Two cokes, one diet you got it," and the waiter was off on his mission.

For over two hours the two talked, first about Bob Wesson and his situation. Sam knew that kind of thing went on all the time in DC, but he didn't have any leads on this particular case. The world of drug money was a little after Sam's time. It was more crimes of lust and hush money, with a little bit of blackmailing politicians back in Sam's day. The era of drug cartels running their own governments, much less having the ability to be powerful enough to run other countries, well, that was a little after Sam's time. But Sam still had contacts. He pulled out a small notepad he always carried and scribbled down a name and phone number. He tore off the piece of paper and handed it to Connie.

"Here, you need to contact this guy, James Bowman. He is an old CIA friend of mine. If something is going on with the Agency, Jimmy will have the skinny on it. If he doesn't he'll still have a name you can contact. Believe me, he will know somebody who might know something about anything. You be sure you tell him Marley sent you. He'll know who you mean. Would you like another coke?"

As time went by the conversation changed to more normal life scenarios as they talked about life and careers such as when Sam was in the army in World War II. He worked alongside with Ernie Pyle, the

Pulitzer Prize winning journalist, and was with him the day he was killed. On and on they talked about when Sam was in the newspaper reporting business, and years of being a private investigator. He also shared the story of when he met Connie's husband Jack, a standout in high school sports.

Sam was doing some sports reporting at the time, plus he knew of Jack's family because he went to school and was a good friend of Jack's father before he was killed in Korea. It was also one of Sam's political friends, a Senator Millhouse, who sponsored Jack so he could attend the Naval Academy in Annapolis and also enter the SEALs program.

Connie knew Jack loved Sam like an uncle, but she never knew all of this. Sam Hornaday was fascinating to Connie; his deep baritone voice was as resonating as that of James Earl Jones, and regardless of his age he was still Sean Connery handsome with combed-back longish gray hair and a thin mustache. His voice and looks were mesmerizing to Connie. She could listen to him all night, and as the waiter came by pointing at his watch for the last time she realized she had.

"It's late Sam and the restaurant is about to close. I could listen to your stories all night long. You are truly great to listen to and I have had the very best time. I'm so glad you did decide to come, but I'm sorry about you getting rained on and everything."

"Connie Womack if I was 20 years younger and you were not married to a dear friend—well all I can say is thank you for wearing that black dress, you look great."

"If you were 20 years younger I would still be married but I have had a great time. You're one interesting man, Sam Hornaday, interesting indeed. Now let me drive you home. It might rain again."

"No thanks, I'll take a cab this time." They both stood up and walked out to the street and stood by the cab stand. "I'll start working for you and Jack first thing in the morning. Trust me, I'll find some dirt to help out your boss, Mr. Wesson. Don't you worry one bit. These streets have answers and I'm the one who can find them for you, pretty lady." With that he leaned down and kissed Connie's hand, turned, and got in a cab and was gone.

Connie shook head in disbelief. *"What a man,"* she thought as she got in her Corvette and drove off.

Sam's cab pulled right up to the wrought-iron gate in front of Sam's loft apartment building. Sam looked up and down the street as he exited the vehicle and quickly noticed the front door of the apartment entrance was wide open. It was not his apartment door but the main entrance door one would use to gain access to one of the eight small apartments inside the building. There were four apartments down and four upstairs. But for the main door to be open like that didn't seem right. He paid the cabbie and proceeded with caution as he slowly walked up the sidewalk. He suddenly stopped and pulled his .38 snub-nosed revolver out of his ankle hoister and began his walk up to the doorway, stopping again to peer inside.

I hate this shit, he thought as he craned his neck and squinted his eyes to see better as he tried to look up the steps to the second-floor landing. He found the light switch along the wall, but the light was broken, and he still couldn't see much of anything. It was way too dark. He quickly stepped inside the doorway and moved into the large foyer. With his back up against the wall he stopped, feeling the mail boxes up against his back. The dim glow from the exit sign gave him enough light so he could quickly check his revolver for ammo. The sound under his feet was that of broken glass that once was the overhead light bulb someone had broken, probably on purpose.

Once he finished inspecting his weapon he proceeded with caution up the stairs to his apartment which was the first door to the right. Methodically, one step at a time, he slowly moved with his back still up against the wall and stayed that way till he made it to the top of the landing. He stopped to catch his breath as he nervously looked down the hallway. All four apartment doors on that floor were closed.

He gave a slight sigh of relief after he walked to his door and found that it was still locked. At this point he was starting to feel a little embarrassed. He may have overreacted. He took another big sigh of relief knowing everything seemed to be OK and put the gun in the back of his pants as he fished in his pockets for his house keys. As he pulled the keys from his pocket they snagged on a loose thread and accidentally dropped to the hall floor.

Damn I hate when that happens he thought, as he bent over to pick up the keys. As he retrieved the keys and stood he unexpectedly heard the squeaky hinges of the door from the apartment across the hall directly behind him opening and in a flash there was a loud bang.

Before Sam could even move the blast from the assassin's bullet hit him from behind and cut right into his back. The blast hit him so hard it threw him up against his own door. He saw the hole in his shirt where the bullet had burst open and outwards as it exited his chest. His body fell with a thud. Pain was running throughout his body, yet he was still alert and cognizant of his actions.

He pulled his revolver from his waistband and tried to focus. Dazed and confused, he was more concerned with why this had just happened to him. Looking down the hall he could see a masked stranger peek out from behind the doorway. Not hesitating, Sam pulled the trigger of his revolver once, then twice. At least one bullet hit the assailant, causing him to fall backward into the apartment.

Sam used this time to once again find his keys, which he saw lying directly at his feet. He fired his gun again into the apartment and quickly turned to finally open his own door, hoping for safe cover, but before he could get inside his loft the second shot came without warning. It hit him in the back for the second time, throwing him forward into his apartment. He landed on his face and knees as he doubled over grabbing his gut.

Sam's mind was now racing, stunned with the thought of dying like this. *Why me and for what, going out to eat?* His breathing became heavy and he labored to inhale and catch his breath. Looking down he noticed his hands shaking badly. He tried to stretch his arm out to retrieve his weapon only inches away from his reach as the assassin approached from the dark.

Sam never heard the third loud bang as his blood splattered over the walls just inside his apartment and out into the hallway. The pain he was suffering with the cancer was now gone, as his blood filled the floor. With his gun still drawn the wounded executioner slowly walked over to check for a pulse. He pressed down feeling for a pulse from the artery in Sam's neck. After the inspection the masked assailant stepped through the blood and over Sam's body, which enabled him to exit the crime scene and escape down the stairs and into the dark of night.

Sam Hornaday's amazing career and life were now over.

Baranski's Bark

Chapter 17

THE OFFICE OF THE DETECTIVE DIVSION of the DC police station was tucked away upstairs on the fifth floor, and sitting in the dark all alone was detective Matt Baranski. He could not believe the news he had just received about his good friend and mentor Sam Hornaday. He stared into the darkness, placing the telephone receiver back on the hook and the phone back on his desk. Sam Hornaday. Sam had helped Matthew, that's what Sam called him by his given name, ever since he was a young kid growing up in a tough neighborhood doing the wrong things like a lot of kids his age and getting into trouble from time to time.

But Matt was not the only one; Sam had helped a lot of lost kids find their way in life. The DC police station was full of the police officers Sam helped make into men. Who would want him dead? Everyone knew Sam was dying. He had fought cancer for a few years now and it was only a matter of time before that would play out. No, it had to be someone Sam knew something on, somebody Sam should not have known or known about. Whatever it was, he paid for it with his life.

The question to Matt was for what? What was the info Sam knew, and who was determined to keep him quiet about it? *It must have been something big,* Matt thought as he remembered long-ago trips he took with Sam to the baseball park to watch Boog Powell and Brooks Robinson, or just a relaxing day of fishing at the old piers along Baltimore's Inner Harbor. Matt had lots of great times as a kid with Sam. He pounded his desk with his fist, as tears rolled down his face, vowing to himself that this case was personal, and he was not about to stop until Sam's killer was apprehended or killed or both. Matt couldn't give a damn at this point as he kicked the trash can across the dark and empty room. But he knew he was going to need some more help, a real professional, someone out of the department, but who?

The first person Matt thought of was Connie. He knew she and Jack liked Sam also. He hated to admit it, but she was the best investigator he knew of, so right then he grabbed the phone once again and dialed her number. He had called it so many times he remembered it by heart. The phone rang and rang but there was no answer. Matt hung up, thought for a second, and then called her again, knowing it was really late but surely she had to wake up. She finally did on the second try.

Connie rubbed her eyes as she looked over at the clock to check the time and read the phone number off her caller ID. "DC police" it read. She sat up in the bed. Tricks jumped on the bed like it was time to get up and eat. She nudged him away as she answered.

"Hello," she said, "can I help you?"

"Connie, it's me, Matt Baranski. I'm sorry Connie, I know it's late but I have bad news."

"Matt, it's three o'clock in the morning. Can't it wait till morning?"

"I thought you might want to know about this, it's Sam, Connie, Sam Hornaday."

"What about Sam? I was just with him for supper last night. Is he OK, is it the cancer, is he in the hospital, what's wrong, Matt?"

"He was murdered tonight at his apartment, shot in the back."

"Murdered—Oh my God, Matt!" she shouted.

"Connie, some son of a bitch killed that sweet old man," said Matt. Connie could hear him crying on the other end of the phone. She couldn't believe it herself as she sat up in bed thinking that it was only a few hours ago that she and Sam were having the time of their lives, not knowing it was going to be his last night on Earth.

"I'll be there in a few minutes. Wait for me."

"There's no need, Connie. The body has already been identified by the officer on duty. You know everyone knew Sam down here at the station. Hell, he raised a lot of us. I just happened to have been here myself working on a case, your case for a matter of fact, when the call came in. I had to be here anyway, meeting with you guys in the morning, so I just decided to stay down here. Heck, I was going to sleep on the old cot in the back room like Sam did so many times. Don't think I'll be doing too much sleeping tonight."

"Yeah, Matt, look—about that meeting with us in the morning?" Then a long pause, Connie didn't say a word. Matt then broke her silence.

"He's going to be a no-show, right? I figured as much."

Connie was surprised he guessed right. "How did you guess that?"

"It makes sense, no subpoena, no perp. But Connie you know I would get a subpoena soon, so why ditch?"

"We're not ditching, Matt. We need a little more time that's all. Remember we are talking about Bob Wesson here."

"I don't give a shit who you're representing, but I will tell you this, if this thing with Sam has to do in any

162

way with your case, then sweetheart the gloves are off, you get me? I'm going to find Sam's killer myself if I have to live in this damn police station. You can bet your pretty sweet ass on that, girlfriend. You will be hearing from me soon," as he slammed the phone receiver down.

"But Matt, we can work together on this." The phone had already gone dead. He never heard Connie's plea as she sat on the side of the bed wondering who in the world would have killed Sam. She knew Matt was just mad and he would get over it. But she also knew full well there was a real good chance it had everything to do with her case. No doubt about it, she thought, a real good chance indeed. There was also a good chance she would not be able to sleep either.

So she got up from the bed. Tricks followed her to the kitchen in hopes of an early meal. Connie opened a can of cat food and filled the bowl, placing the bowl on the floor for Tricks to partake. She moved to the table and sat, thinking of Sam. *I need to call Jack. If the timing is right, he'll want to go to the funeral. And then there's Bob and Nancy. What the hell am I going to do with them? If someone killed Sam, surely Bob is next. I'm surprised they didn't get him first. Maybe old Bob is not telling me everything about this CIA deal. I may have to make an early house call on old Bob and Nancy Wesson.*

Connie pulled out one of her notepads and started to write down a few questions using a time line. *What time was it when Bob called her? Who was the dead guy on the floor really and what about his wife and that crazy insurance policy?* Connie worked on the case all night. By morning she was through as she read back over the many pages of notes in her notepad. With a sigh she got up from the table and walked over to turn on the coffee pot for the third time. Grabbing the notepad she reread her notes as she walked into the bathroom to shower, knowing she was ready.

Game Changer

Chapter 18

BOTH WESSONS SAT ON THE COUCH LOOKING UP at Connie wondering why the early morning visit? Rhys Garret wondered the same thing, as morning came way too early to everyone in the safehouse, including Connie who had the least amount of sleep of anyone.

"Bob, I need some answers from you this morning and I don't want to hear anymore lies or half-truths but straight direct answers, do you understand me?"

Bob was surprised at her tone toward him; he had never been anything but good and kind to Connie

Womack. He gave her this job for Christ sake. He was good friends with her husband, Jack. And now he felt betrayed by her questioning his loyalty, and why now?

"Connie, I have answered your questions. Hell, I gave you some answers to questions without you even asking. I don't understand your tone. You are acting like you don't trust me anymore, and to tell you the truth, Connie, that hurts."

Connie walked over closer to the Wessons and sat in the white chair directly in front of the two. She looked at Nancy with empathy, knowing she didn't have a clue. Then she quickly turned and faced Bob once again. "Bob to tell you the truth right now I don't give a shit that I might be hurting your damn feelings. I'm sorry if you feel that way, but here is what I know. My boss calls me to come down to his office because there was a dead man lying on the floor that he hardly knew anything about. I was told by you that a couple of days earlier the dead man's wife came to the same office and wanted to purchase a $10 million life insurance policy on this man you told the police you did not know. Should I continue?"

"Wait Connie, I can explain," Bob shouted.

Connie then raised her hand as to have permission to talk. "Oh no Bob, I'm not finished. You just wait a minute. You will have your time, trust me. Now where was I?" Connie glared at Nancy and Bob. "Yes, you then told me after we left the police and went inside another office that you did know the dead guy and not only knew him, but you two worked for the CIA on occasions."

"The CIA! Bob, what's this all about?" Nancy shouted this time.

"That's right, Nancy, that CIA, the Central Intelligence Agency of the United States of America, the big boys we call them." Connie looked back down at her notes again.

"Here's where it gets sticky. You say the FBI agents were being killed off by some rogue CIA agents so no one would find out about these so-called drug cartels from Columbia smuggling thousands of pounds of pure cocaine via Venezuela into the country, is that right?" Bob shook his head in the affirmative. "So answer me this one Bob, if that story is true and all these people are dying to keep this all a big secret, then why was I told just last night at dinner that this kind of thing happens all the time. And not only that, lots of folks knew about this particular shipment, which has been going on for years now. Answer me that, Mr. Wesson."

"I don't know Connie, maybe your source is wrong, maybe that old man did not know what he was talking about?" Suddenly all eyes turned toward Bob.

Rhys stood up and Connie could not believe her own ears. She too stood up and walked away from the couch. Her mind was racing. She apparently didn't really know this man she worked for all these years. He was definitely not the man she thought she knew.

Connie started her questioning again, this time in a very calm and methodical voice.

"I didn't say who my sources were Bob, so how did you know that I got my information from an older man? And not just a man, but **that** old man, I believe was your exact answer. Now would you like to elaborate on who you think that old man was?"

Connie's tone quickly changed as she started to shout. "And I say the word **was** because the sweet, wonderful old man that I had dinner with last night was shot in the back and killed when he arrived at his apartment after leaving me only 30 minutes earlier! Now you tell me what the hell you know, and you tell me now," as Connie pulled her snub-nosed .357 out of her pocket. Nancy started to scream when she saw the gun.

"Now Connie, wait!" shouted Bob. "No, no, please Connie I had nothing to do with his death. Now that's a fact, now put down that gun!" he shouted.

"Connie, he's right. You can't do this, please put the gun down," said Rhys as he walked over to Connie and reached out for the weapon. "Now please give me the gun, Connie. This is not the way."

Nancy screamed even louder as Connie pointed the gun straight at Bob Wesson's head. Connie would not listen to either one as she demanded an answer. "Who set us up Bob? You better tell me. I'm not messing around here, damn you. Now tell me who killed my friend you son of a bitch," as her eyes filled with tears.

"Tell me, I mean it," she shouted once more as she pulled back on the trigger and the cylinder turned in position ready to fire.

Without saying a word Bob Wesson sat straight up on the couch as calm and collected as anyone Rhys had ever seen in combat. Bob stood up and looked Connie straight in the eye with the gun still pointed straight at his forehead.

"I am so sorry about your loss last night, Connie, but you have to believe me, I'm not the enemy here. I knew Sam too, Connie, he was like a brother to me. We were both dear friends and coworkers. For years we traded information back and forth and tried to watch out for each other, so I guess in a way you're right, but before you pull that trigger, Sam told me to tell you that Marley sent me."

"Marley sent you?" Connie could not believe she was hearing the words Sam told her. "How do you know that name Marley, Bob? Sam told me his friend's name was James Bowman."

"Yeah, but to always call on Marley when you get into trouble, right, wasn't that what Sam told you, Connie?"

Connie stood there with a shocking look still on her face. Bob's eyes were filling with tears as he reached out and took the gun from Connie. The two embraced in a much-needed hug, as Bob then whispered in her ear.

"Connie, 'Marley' wasn't ever a person, it was our code word. Sam and I used it as a safety precaution.

If either one of us was to get in trouble we were to use that code name. My given name is James Robert Bowman. That's the name I used when I first worked for the agency. Later I changed it to Robert Wesson as an alias, and through the years I kept it. My friends call me Bob." As the two were still hugging Rhys reached around the two and slowly removed the gun from Bob's hand as the two finished their embrace and mourned over their lost friend.

Nancy slumped back into the couch and breathed a sigh of relief. She too knew her part in these charades, but she had grown callus to it and besides, they had been happily married for years, so to her it worked. But even to her this was a bit too much as she stood up and headed to the bar. "I know it's early in the morning, but I believe I'll have a drink. Would anyone like to join me?" Nancy asked, as she walked over to the bar in the corner of the large white room.

"No thank you, Nancy, answered Connie, but I still have a few more questions, Bob. Like when did you and Sam decide to bring me in on this case? And why now, if you were in so deep why would you risk losing your cover?"

"Because of Sam I did it," he said. "Sam never knew anything about it, it was all my doings. I couldn't stand it any longer, and I was not about to let him go out like that. Besides he was the best of the best and he loved the game and was damn good at it, but after that horrible fight with cancer I'm afraid he just gave up. I was hoping this case would give him something to live for, at least for a little longer anyway. But I had no idea someone would kill him and this soon. I should have warned him of the danger sooner. It is my fault."

"It's not your fault, Bob, but how did you know I would call him for help?"

"I know how Jack thinks and I knew if I got you two involved sooner or later Sam Hornaday would be called into action. But now the problem, I'm afraid, is that you and Jack are involved as well, and trust me, Connie, these are people you do not want to mess with."

"Well, that's just great Bob, thanks again. And yes Nancy, I believe I'll take that drink now!"

Bob looked over at Connie, still trying to convince her. "Now wait a minute, Connie, it's going to be OK. I figure between Jack and his army of men, plus your brains, we can handle this situation. The only problem is will Jack help? I'll need your help on that one."

Rhys broke his silence as he turned around to face Bob. "After you just got his wife involved in a double murder I don't believe that will be your only problem, Mr. Wesson. Jack will be pissed, and I'm a little upset my damn self."

"And you can believe that," Connie said across the room at the bar. "But hey, you won't have long to find out. I told Jack about Sam and yes, he will be here for the funeral. You can talk to him then. It's a good thing you're in a safehouse Bob, because I'm afraid when Jack gets home you are going to definitely need it as protection," Connie warned as she finished her first drink. "Nancy, make me another vodka tonic please," as she raised her glass in Nancy's direction.

"Hell, make it two," said Rhys.

Bob walked over to the bar. "Might as well make it three more drinks sweetheart."

The
Prisoner

Chapter 19

THE MORNING SUN WAS ON ITS RISE AS THE ONCE FAINT LIGHT slowly but surely grew stronger and brighter, as a new day dawned. The sun's rays crested over the horizon as it quickly raced across the landscape of roads and fields, both warming and illuminating all it touched. The running beams of light then abruptly bent upward as they hit and run up the 40-foot stone wall.

And like a burglar the light sneaked up the detainment wall as it started to peek into the small and narrow slit of a window, arriving in prison cell 14 as it did every morning. That one single beam of powerful light suddenly lit up the whole jail cell, simultaneously striking a pain in the open eyes of the prisoner with a surprise attack as he lay wide awake on his small bunk with his feet dangling off the end.

"Damn it!" He instantly turned his head away and placed his hands over his tightly closed eyes, which had been wide open as the sunlight filled the room. As the pain subsided he thought of the reason he could not sleep, his mind and eyes fixated on the ceiling while he was in deep thought, remembering why he was here in the first place. *Damn is right* he thought. Damn the morning light, damn this Fort Leavenworth prison, and damn that Jack Womack, the son of a bitch that put me in here in the first place.

His thoughts of hate in his heart had spilled out of his mouth. "I haven't forgotten your ass, Commander Womack," he said aloud, "and don't worry, I'll get that little wife of yours too, so help me." All six feet six inches of Cecil Locklear then rolled his legs off the end of the bunk and he sat up facing away from the window to hide his eyes from the sun's light as he welcomed a new day in his self-made hell.

This prison at Fort Leavenworth, Kansas, was no regular penitentiary. No, this was the United States Disciplinary Barracks (USDB), unofficially called the Castle. It was the only maximum-security penitentiary within the Department of Defense and was only one of four prisons located at Fort Leavenworth. But the USDB, or the Castle, housed some of the worst of the worst the military had to offer.

For the most severe prisoner there was special solitary confinement housing reserved for a select few. These inmates could be locked in their cell up to 23 hours a day. Their food arrived through a small slot at the bottom door. A small peephole in the door let the guards, or correctional specialists as they were called, keep an eye on the prisoners at all times. And if, or when, the inmate did get permission to leave his cell, the correctional specialists chained the inmate's ankles together before he was escorted out to take a shower or to get some fresh air. As they said in the Castle, "There's not but two kinds of soldiers, those without rank and pay and those with keys."

Cecil rubbed his eyes as he thought to himself. *At least he had a window. After all most folks who get into a knife fight in this prison usually would get six months if not longer in solitary confinement with no window. So somebody does like me.* Hearing a sound he turned to the sound of the voice on the other side of the door.

"Hey, Locklear, you up?" questioned the correctional specialist standing just outside his cell door.

"No, I'm asleep, asshole, can't you tell?"

"Hey, don't get smart with me, Chief; I'm just here with some good news, alright?"

"Yeah, sure sorry boss, what is it?" Cecil asked as he moved closer to the cell door to hear his newfound friend better.

"They tell me the warden is going to let you out of here early. Now I heard this through the grapevine

175

and I don't know when exactly, but I think pretty soon. It looks like your new attorney did something or the bigwigs must like you. Whatever the case, you need to keep your big mouth shut and watch your ass. The boys back home might have a job for you when you get out of here, so keep it cool, Chief."

"What, a job? What the hell are you talking about, boys back home?" he asked. "Hey man, I'm talking to you," but there was no reply. "Hey wait a minute." But it was too late. The mystery guard had already left, leaving Cecil to just sit back on his bunk in his cell and wonder about all kinds of questions, curiosity running through his mind.

Years in prison caused a man to hone his thinking skills as Cecil calmly sat on his bunk with his back against the wall, trying to understand the meaning to the guard's intentions. He knew his time at the Castle was ending in a few years but not this soon. And why now, and why would someone or a group of people feel as though they needed to tell him in prison of all places? And what was this great plan they had in store for him? Suddenly his thoughts were stopped by the sound of another guard.

"Breakfast, asshole," the guard shouted, as a tray of food slid through the small opening at the bottom of the door.

"Great, the start of a nutritious day with a wholesome and healthy portion of slop," said Cecil out loud as he stood up and leaned over to retrieve his breakfast. Quickly he sat back down and after inspecting the plate of food he started devouring it as fast as possible, holding his breath at the same time. This was his effort to avoid and disregard the taste altogether.

It wasn't until he was through eating and started to use his napkin to wipe his mouth that he noticed some writing on the paper. At first he thought it was a bug or something, but then he noticed it was a name in small print written on the napkin, only one name and an initial—Godfrey B. Quickly. Cecil gobbled up the small piece of paper in his mouth as if it was an after-dinner mint and washed it down with a cool drink of water, leaving no evidence or proof that he had been contacted by anyone.

"Delicious," he said with a smile on his face knowing now, after almost ten years, he was not alone and soon to be free. For years he had waited for an answer from somebody. He could not believe it had taken this long.

Ten long years he had been sentenced to 2nd degree murder for killing Steven Hyatt, a Delta Special Forces member, in the first days of the first Iraq war in 1991. The court-martial was based on the single testimony of Cecil's superior officer, Commander Jack Randall Womack, stating that Cecil Locklear single-handedly killed one of his men in cold blood, and that it was not in the line of duty as Cecil and specialist Thomas Wise had suggested.

Another strange occurrence and pure luck for Cecil was that every witness of that event suddenly and mysteriously died, either in action on the battlefield or accidentally when they returned to the states. Jack Womack was furious, thinking how convenient it was that the witnesses were not able to testify, and knowing full well that Cecil had something to do with those deaths. But regardless of the prosecutor's objections the court had no choice but to lessen Cecil's charges to second degree with a sentence of 10 to 20 years. And for almost 10 years Cecil was in and out of solitary confinement due to his own doings, regardless that he blamed Jack for every minute he was in prison.

A born leader, Cecil Locklear was ruthless and very cunning. His skill at mind manipulation was incredible and no one seemed to be immune to it, especially the worst of the worst. Cecil's plan was to convert sadistic, criminal-minded people over to his way of thinking, making him in charge.

Sure, over the years he had been challenged, but he was willing to stamp out those challengers even if he had to visit solitary confinement every now and then. But to this point after all these years, Cecil had amassed a small army of criminals at his disposal. Thieves, murderers, and rapists, all vowed their devotion and were willing to do just about anything he told them to do. The key to his plan was to find prisoners whose sentences were as short, if not shorter, than his so they would already be on the outside and at the ready to serve when he called.

Cecil Locklear, aka Chief, was truly a madman with a diabolical but brilliant mind who could manipulate just about anyone he wanted, and everything he did was calculated. His years in the military were no different; he stole thousands of dollars in drugs, gold, silver, and artifacts. And the only one man that stopped him was retired Commander Jack Randall Womack who was now in his sights.

All Cecil could think about was revenge. Regardless of who or what group of people just hired him he would act as if he was now at their mercy. At least that was what Cecil wanted them to believe. Sure, he would do whatever they asked, just long enough till his plan was in place. After all, no one told Cecil Locklear what to do. A smile formed on his face as he lay on the small bed. He then heard the sound of metal hitting metal. Keys rattled in the lock, and his cell door slowly opened.

"Locklear, let's go, up and at 'em, out! Come on boy, your time is up. You're going back to general population," shouted the guard. Cecil's smile grew even larger knowing someone was watching out for him.

Jack's Arrival

Chapter 20

THE SKY WAS DARK WITH LARGE GRAY CLOUDS, the rain pouring down in sheets across the runway. Rhys turned toward Connie with a carafe of coffee, offering her another cup as she peered out at the rain and through the small window in Jack's office at the small municipal airport located just outside of Washington, DC.

"Here you are, Connie," said Rhys, as she turned around long enough for him to fill her cup. Then turning her attention back to the weather, she waited patiently for the rain to stop but she felt the rain was a fitting omen after all she had gone through in the last 24 hours. Seeing the rain slow down made her feel slightly better knowing Jack would soon be landing, but her thoughts were still about Sam. She never really knew Sam Hornaday that well, but she knew now she would always miss him dearly, as she accepted the second cup of java from Rhys.

"Connie, do you ever think about the times you and I dated before Jack came into your life? I wonder if you and I would have ever gotten married, you know?"

"Married, are you kidding me? Rhys, you have never dated the same girl more than three times in your life and you know it. It takes more than just sex for a good relationship, and that's why there's a good chance you'll never be ready for a long-term commitment, much less marriage.

"Hey, I can change, you never know, Connie, one of these days."

"To be honest, I'd rather you be my best friend, plus if you remember, we went out what two times, three maybe, and you know it didn't work out. No, you stick with being yourself, the ladies' man that you are, and I'll stay married to Jack. How's that?"

"Sorry, I was just thinking."

"Well, quit thinking, you're not too good at that anyway, and now let me know how the weather is looking on that radar screen," she said, as the beeping sound coming from the weather satellite monitor made them both turn their attention to the big green blot. More weather was moving over the Washington, DC, metro area but the good news was that the worst of the weather was away from their location and the small airport where Jack was about to land.

Rhys realized Connie did not want to talk any more about their past and quickly put his attention back on Jack's arrival. "She's clearing up over Delaware and that's a good sign, Connie," as he pointed to the open area on the monitor and a small smile appeared on her lips. She could not wait to see her Jack, but her mind and heart were still elsewhere, and she would not let Sam's passing go without the proper condolences as a tear ran down her cheek.

"You know, Rhys, I'm really going to miss that Sam. That old man was one of a kind and truly a real gentleman. I bet he was a real ladies' man back in his day. Rhys nodded yes, as they both sat and watched the rain pour down outside.

"Yeah, he was something else from what Jack used to say about the guy. He was truly an original and the ladies did love him. That was one of his problems with his first two wives," he said with a slight laugh. "Did you know he was knighted by the Queen of England? Yeah, he received a metal or something by the Queen."

"No, are you kidding? That's a pretty big deal. I didn't know any of that."

"To be honest I can't remember exactly whether he was knighted or received some kind of medal, something like that, but it had to do with him writing a newspaper article about kids getting killed and hurt in Northern Ireland. Yeah, his investigative reporting on Northern Ireland helped save a bunch of children from getting killed or something like that. Anyway, he loved to help kids. You need to ask Jack to tell you those old stories about Sam."

Suddenly the radio came to life as the noise of a jet blew by the line shack and Jack's airplane was spotted making a pass-over by both Rhys and Connie. Rhys turned to Connie as they watched the plane fly out of sight. "Looks like you get your chance sooner than later." They both got up from the desk and walked over to the door to greet her husband and his boss.

"Fairview tower this is Beechcraft 9-1-7 Alfa Romeo Victor requesting to land, over," as the radio in the line shack crackled with Jack's voice.

"Roger that, Beechcraft 9-1-7, runway 18 is clean and green. You have permission to land, over."

Connie looked at the radio and then at Rhys. "There are only two landing strips out there Rhys, so what's with runway 18?" Rhys laughed, explaining that airport runways are named by a number between 01 and 36, which is generally the magnetic azimuth of the runway's heading in deka or decadegrees. A runway number 09 points east at 90 degrees, and a runway numbered 18 is south at 180 degrees. Connie appreciated the lesson and turned back around to watch the landing, listening to the radio at the same time.

"Roger that Fairview tower, this is Beechcraft 9-1-7 Alfa Romeo Victor lining up for final approach."

Suddenly the aircraft's wings dipped to the right and back to the left as it lined up the airport's runway on its final approach. The whizzing sound of the landing gear started as the doors slowly opened causing the aircraft's speed to quickly decrease even more as the plane's altitude rapidly dropped as well. Within a minute or two Connie and Rhys noticed the brightness of the landing lights, the rays piercing through the rain and clouds on its final approach from the south.

Jack throttled back the airspeed which was now less than 140 knots, and he steadily decreased its air speed, making the aircraft appear to be floating on air like a kite. Within a couple of seconds Connie and Rhys witnessed the familiar sight and sounds of the tires barking as the rubber tires hit the runway accompanied with a large puff of blue smoke.

"Fairview tower, Beechcraft 9-1-7, Alfa Romeo Victor is home once again with a safe landing and we thank you for your assignations and help, over."

"Roger that Jack, welcome home 9-1-7, glad you boys made it back home safe and sound, this is Fairview tower, over and out."

The incoming Hawker Beechcraft Horizon aircraft made its way down the runway and after a couple of quick right and left turns it proceeded to taxi down and across the tarmac heading straight for the line shack where Connie and Rhys were commiserating over Sam as they waited for Jack to deplane.

"I wonder how much Jack knows about his friend Bob Wesson."

"Well, we are getting ready to find out," Connie said as the sleek black jet aircraft with the company's logo DPS Security in bold gold print covering the length of the fuselage pulled right up to the building. The once loud sound of the roaring jet engines abruptly stopped, and the engines were turned to the off position. The slow unwinding process began as each turn of the turbines slowed and finally stopped altogether. Connie could see Jack in the pilot's seat going through his deplaning procedures, marking off his checklist as fast as he could.

Several of his men made it down the steps as Connie waited patiently.

"Hey, Connie, sorry about Sam, he was a good man," said Spider Rountree as he walked off the stairs and gave her a hug.

"Thanks, Sydney." The two hugged as several more men deplaned. Finally, off the plane came her Jack and Connie ran over to meet him. She fell into his arms and the two kissed.

Rhys stood patiently waiting as the two embraced as though they had been separated for a year or two. "Damn you two! He was only gone for three days this time, Connie."

The two stopped their embrace long enough to look up at Rhys, turning and speaking at the same time. "Jealous!"

"Maybe, but late is more like it, Jack. We need to go if we are going to make it to Sam's funeral."

"Sam would understand, besides he's not going anywhere."

Connie pulled back from her husband in shock. "Jack, that's a terrible thing to say."

"Maybe, but what is really terrible is that some son of a bitch came in off the street and shot and killed one of my best friends and there was nothing I could do about it." And with that they got in the car and drove away.

The gray and rainy day felt appropriate to Connie for Sam's funeral. The large crowd was very diverse, which included police personnel, city officials, old newspaper reporters and editors he had and had not worked with, plus a couple of TV news anchors, David Brinkley and Frank Reynolds. There was also a large group of young and old from the Big Brothers Big Sisters of America organization, which Sam helped start up and run for years.

The rain did not let up as the crowd closely huddled under umbrellas, and the ones without tried to escape the rain by doing their best to fit under the only funeral tent. The young priest read the scriptures as if he remembered Sam back in the days when he frequented the church. But there were no such days in the life of Sam Hornaday, and it became pretty clear that he and the priest were strangers. Those who did know Sam knew that he felt it was more important to live the Christian life than to show up at a building. With the amount of people that came out to his funeral, there was no doubt many loved the man, as the rain drops helped mask their tears.

"Ashes to ashes and dust to dust, amen," the priest declared, and the eclectic crowd began to disperse. Jack noticed Detective Matt Baranski as he and a few other cops were headed off to their vehicles.

"Honey, I'll be right back," said Jack as he kissed Connie on the cheek and headed in their direction calling out Matt's name. Matt, hearing his name, turned to see the caller.

"Hey, Jack, see you finally made it back to the states." He stopped and faced Jack as he walked down the hill from the gravesite.

"Hello, Matt, see you finally made detective."

Matt's expression turned cold as he looked back at Jack. "What do you want from me, Womack? I thought you were having your wife do all your leg work these days?"

"Look Matt, I came over to say hello. After all we both loved that old man. I only came over to say hello and to see how you are doing, that's all."

"Yeah, and maybe ask if we have found out anything on Sam's case?"

"Yeah maybe, just want to help," Jack replied.

"I tell you what Jack, you get that wife of yours to give up my witness and I'll see if there's any new information my department has on our dead friend, deal?"

"I don't know what you are talking about, Baranski, but if she knows anything I'll call you back."

"You do that, commander. I look forward to the phone call. Now you have a nice day and enjoy this rain." With that he and the rest of the policemen who were with him walked off. Connie walked up behind Jack in time to barely hear the end of the conversation.

"Jack, is everything alright with you two?"

"Yeah, everything is the same as it was before. I don't understand why that guy hates me so much. Hell, we were friends when we grew up together. I can't figure him out—but the heck with him. Let's go to Baltimore and have a little talk with our friend Bob before we have to hand him back over to mister nice guy Baranski."

"I think you are right, but I also believe we need to do a little more research before we head back down and scare the heck out of Bob and Nancy again."

"Again? You have already been back to question Bob about Sam's death and you didn't tell me?"

"Well, Jack it's been a little busy around here to say the least with everything going on, but yes, Rhys and I went and had a word with Mr. Wesson, and it

188

turns out that old Sam and Bob worked together for years as undercover operatives for the CIA."

"Bob Wesson worked for the CIA? Wow, I've known Bob for years and had no idea he worked for the agency. I suspected Sam did. He worked for everybody. But now you tell me that both dear friends of mine were operatives on the inside of the CIA. Next you're going to tell me that Bob Wesson isn't his real name."

"You're right, Jack," she said with hesitation and a kiss on the cheek.

ASININE ASSASSIN

Chapter 21

THE DOOR OPENED TO A SMALL DARK ROOM as a person hurriedly stepped in and quickly shut the door behind. Out of breath, he used the door to lean against as he stood there sweating and trying to catch his breath, his heart pounding in his chest. Holding his right arm he then turned back around and took a look back through the peephole, checking to see if the coast was clear. After a short time he was convinced he was not followed.

The pain in his arm intensified as he turned away from the door and quickly moved through the apartment. He clumsily knocked over a floor lamp as he threw his torn and wet raincoat into the corner chair causing his black ski mask to fall out, as he headed straight to the bathroom.

He flipped the light switch to the on position and headed over to the medicine cabinet. Blood was running down his right arm and began to splatter into a pool on the black and white checkered tile floor. He turned on the hot water faucet and turned back as he continued his reach into the cabinet while the water had time to heat up. Suddenly the items he was looking for finally appeared, as one by one he lay them out on the bathroom counter. He struggled to remove his blood-soaked shirt. Once it was removed he threw it on the floor with a wet and loud thud. He checked the temperature of the water before he cupped some up into his hand, bending over the sink in an attempt to clear out the wound.

"Oh God," he shouted as he banged his fist on the counter. With one hand he removed the bottle's cap and poured. The pain became so intense he bit down on his lip and continued to clean out the wound with alcohol. He felt as though he might either pass out, throw-up, or both. He stopped for a few minutes as he gathered both his nerve and his breath, and while he rested he placed a wash towel between his bloody lips.

The thought of his next move suddenly caused his hands to shake uncontrollably. His mind was on fire as he was finally able to pick up the pair of tweezers.

Holding both the tweezers and his breath at the same time, he began to anticipate the unbearable pain as his moaning slowly increased into a muffled scream.

Suddenly with one quick move he thrust the tweezers into the opening in his arm like a dart. Beads of sweat appeared on his forehead immediately as he continued his exploratory surgery. The pain was overwhelming as he pulled the instrument out long enough to catch his breath. Tears filled his eyes and he felt faint but he couldn't stop at this point. He once again impaled himself as he continued to fish between the deltoid and tricep muscles for the foreign debris.

Then unexpectedly he felt something deep between the two muscles. *Is this it?* he prayed. It's got to be, he thought, as the object seemed to move and twist away from the tweezers. Again he stopped to regroup. He reapplied the alcohol by splashing the liquid on his arm. Hovering over the sink he held his breath as he once again readied himself for battle.

His mind took over and without warning he plunged the metal tweezers to their deepest depth. Then once more he stabbed into his flesh, then twice, and then a third time. He fell to his knees as the tweezers lessened its grab and he dropped the .357 slug of metal into the sink with the water still running.

Exhausted and completely spent, he managed to remove the towel from his mouth and used it to apply pressure to the wound. Slowly he began to slide down off the cabinet onto the cold, blood-drenched floor. He closed his eyes and passed out.

Hours must have passed before he opened his eyes. Questions raced back through his mind. His hand was still holding the towel on his arm. He puzzled how he got into this mess in the first place, but the sense of cold from the floor enticed him to try to sit up. Slowly he worked his way up and started to stand, finally getting his feet under him.

He noticed more towels and gauze sitting on the counter and he began to dress the wound. Unexpectedly the phone beside the bed rang. With a shocked look on his face he wondered what to do. *Nobody knows I'm here*, he thought. *Hell, I didn't know this place even had a phone.* The phone continued ringing as he hoped that it would soon stop, and after a few more rings it did.

He welcomed the silence with a sigh of relief as he quickly grabbed more towels and started to clean off the dried blood on his arm. Again it started, the insistent ringing. Ring after ring, this time it would not stop as minutes went by. *Do I answer it or not* runs through his mind until the repetitive noise finally causes him to put an end to the aggravating sound by picking up the receiver.

"Hello," he answered as he waited for a reply. Again he spoke to the unknown, "Hello, who is this?".

"Now, now Monsieur, do not get so upset," said the voice with the familiar French accent. "Everything is fine; I'm calling to see if you are alright after your assignment and to congratulate you on a job well done."

"Sure, I'm great, thanks for the love there, Frenchie. You don't have to send flowers, I'm doing fine, thanks for asking."

"Well my job is to help assist whenever it is necessary. Now again do you need anything? Are you injured in anyway, do you need medical services?

"I said no, asshole, I'm just fine. And don't you ever call me here again. Do you understand me, damn it, never call me again," he shouted as he hung up the phone.

Quickly the ring rang again and just like last time the ringing would not stop till he answered. He finally caved in again.

"Monsieur, as you Americans say, I will let that one go. This is one time only but do not test me again while I'm talking do you. Do you understand me? I know it's been years since we have met but just to be clear of who I represent, I know that you work for Monsieur Cecil, but you see Monsieur Cecil works for us. That means you work for us and the organization likes things done neat with no loose strings. Again I ask if you are wounded and if so, you have the number we gave you to call for help and I insist you use it, please. Do you understand me now?"

"I understand," said Skeeter.

"Now don't forget Monsieur, we have people everywhere and we know everything about our people like yourself, Mr. Thomas Wise, or do you prefer your nickname? Skeeter, is it?"

Skeeter was shocked when he heard his name, almost dropping the phone.

"So please believe me, Skeeter, when I say if you need help please call. We want to keep you healthy. You are no good to us if you bleed to death on that bathroom floor. Now you take care."

Skeeter again was shocked by what the man said. He looked around the room feeling as though someone was watching him as the phone suddenly went dead.

"Hello, hello," he shouted into the phone receiver but there was nothing but dial tone as the infamous Frenchman was gone, and without question he got his point across.

Skeeter began to panic as he started looking around the small apartment for a camera. He ran his fingers over picture frames, doorframes, and windowsills. He turned over tables, the couch, chairs, even the small bed in the back room. Pillows, mattresses, seat cushions. He didn't stop till the room looked like a bomb had gone off in it.

He looked around the room long enough to catch his breath and examine his handiwork as his arm started bleeding again. He applied more pressure to the wound while wondering if he should make the phone call for medical help. The hell with it! His head was still spinning from the whole ordeal as he stood there looking at the wrecked apartment. "*What the hell has Cecil got me into this time?*"

THE ROUND TABLE

Chapter 22

ALL FOUR SAT AT THE KITCHEN TABLE WONDERING what their next move would be in solving this crazy case. Everyone seemed to be in a deep train of thought. Both Rhys and Kay had finished their notes while Connie was still writing down a few more lines on the yellow pages in her notebook. Her mind was still on Bob, wanting to have another crack at talking to him. Both she and Kay agreed that he had to be up to something more. His story or stories just didn't add up. There had to be something else he was hiding according to both Kay's and Connie's intuitions. They were sure of it.

Jack, on the other hand, kept writing in his notes. The other three patiently ate popcorn and watched and waited for several minutes as Jack continued to write. Rhys, however, was tired of the whole thing and was ready to beat the heck out of anyone who could tell them anything at all. He was sick of the whole thing, and at this point, nothing made any sense to him.

"Come on guys, let's go back over to the safehouse and beat the shit out of that Wesson guy. You know he is lying. How about we just pull a GITMO on his ass and get a few answers out of him. I know I can get him to talk."

"Guantanamo Bay Detention Center, what are you, Mr. Waterboarder at camp GITMO now or something?" said Connie with a laugh. They all looked over at Rhys as if he was crazy.

Jack finally finished and laid the pen down. "OK, here's how I see it. First, I believe a few things are going on and that's the main reason why nothing seems to be making any sense. There's more than one case going on here. That's why it appears to be so complicated but it's not that complicated really. You remove some of the factors going on all at once and it's clear we're working on two, if not three different cases. Sure, there are some of the same actors, but it's sounding too bizarre to me, again too complicated."

"So how do you suggest we approach it?" said Kay as she too felt overwhelmed.

"You're saying we need to break it down and each of us take part, a person who we believe is involved. You never know where that may lead us," said Connie.

"Yeah, like for example, it's hard for me to believe that Sam's death and Bob's CIA case are related," said Jack. "Sure Bob knew Sam, but hell, half the police station and anyone who read the news in the last 40 years knew Sam Hornaday. There has to be something that ties Bob or Sam, or that IT guy and his wife, with someone else. We understand that and I believe we will have this thing figured out."

"What are you saying? You think there is a link that will prove Bob Wesson is a murderer?"

"No, I'm not saying he killed anyone. I'm just saying that there's more than one case here, and we need to separate the two, if not the three, from each other before we can go much further, that's all."

Connie moved her chair back a little from the table and spoke. "OK, then we will need to understand who the players are. We have Bob Wesson, who called me saying he needed help and to come to his office. Later we find out that there was a dead guy in the office and Bob lied to the police and later told Kay and me a different story all together."

"Now wait, we got Bob and a dead IT guy. What's his name?" asked Jack.

"Daniel Gambo, no, it's Gambaro, and his wife's name is Kim I think," answered Kay.

Rhys looked up at Jack. "Now don't forget Matt Baranski. I don't trust that guy. He's an asshole."

"Rhys, that guy's a decorated police detective. He's really a good guy, Rhys, you need to loosen up a little. What is it with you and cops anyway. He's alright. I bet if you got to know him you would like him. Plus he grew up with Jack. Trust me, he is OK," said Connie.

Jack was still mad at Matt from the funeral as he shrugged his shoulders with his answer, which wasn't much of an endorsement. "He's alright I guess."

"All I'm saying is there is always one bad cop in the bunch, and if not him it will be another one, trust me. Maybe that sidekick of his, that Riddle fella? Hey, I'm just saying."

"Tommy Riddle? Are you crazy? He's one of the nicest guys you'll ever meet," answered Connie.

"Let's get back on subject please," Jack asked, "and no speculations, we need the facts. Be it cops or whoever. I want each one of you to compile a list of names of people that you believe need to be checked out, and I don't care the reason, it could be only a hunch, that's fine. And don't worry if we come up with any duplicate names. We'll go through and sort the list out and remove any duplicates. After that you will be assigned to that one person. So how about we meet back here tomorrow morning and start fresh?"

"That sounds good to me," said Kay, as Connie too agreed by nodding her head.

"Yeah me too," replied Rhys, who was totally and completely bored out of his mind and basically was tired of sitting there doing nothing for hours. He slowly stood up and with his hands on his waist he gradually bent backwards and then leaned forward, in an effort to stretch out his back and legs. Everyone watched Rhys as he continued his stretching at a snail's pace away from the table. He placed his hand over his mouth trying to keep from yawning.

"He looks like a big old bear awakening from hibernation," Kay commented.

Then Jack suddenly spoke up as the girls were all watching Rhys as he stretched and pulled on his legs and arms. "That must be it!" Jack shouted."

"Must be what, honey?" Connie questioned.

"A sleeper cell of some kind, that's the only answer. Somebody has awakened a sleeper cell, and Bob or Sam, hell even one of us, may be the target. That's why nothing is making sense. There has to be a third party pulling someone's strings. And by the way, thanks for that yawn, Rhys."

"You're welcome I guess," he said, not having a clue what Jack was talking about and at that point of the night he didn't care.

Kay laughed and looked over at Rhys. "Come on Smoky Bear, I'll take you home. We'll see everyone in the morning at the airport." The two walked out the backdoor.

"Be careful you two," said Connie, as Jack waved. Connie quickly turned back around and faced Jack. "You really believe we could be targeted as well, Jack?" Connie said with concern in her voice.

"Baby, all I'm saying is that there could be a third party, maybe some kind of group or organization, heck it could be the neo-Nazis. We do not know anything at this time, that's all. But we'll find them, so don't worry. You and I are OK. Now let's go to bed. We have more important things to do before we sleep."

"You are all talk, big man, all talk," as the two went running up the stairs laughing with Tricks in tow.

Short-Timer

Chapter 23

THE LIGHTS FLASHED AND THE AIRHORN SOUNDED the alarm as the whole prison was placed on lockdown. Prisoners ran to the safety of their cells while correctional guards arrived in large forces. The sound of metal doors being shut and locked in place could be heard as guards marched with batons and truncheon clubs in hand at the ready. Two prisoners remained, who were wrestling on the hard concrete floor of the military prison in Fort Leavenworth, Kansas. The correctional guards stood there forming a circle corralling the two like mustang horses, confining them to the one small area of the prison as more guards stood on the mezzanine overlooking the fight from above. The cries of pain were heard throughout the prison.

"I don't care if it hurts or not you son of a bitch. I'm in charge, you hear me?" shouted Cecil as he had the man's arm bent over his leg, threatening to break it.

"Please don't, Chief, O God, I won't do it again I promise, please don't break my arm, please," the man shouted. Suddenly the large Indian known as Chief stopped. After all, he only wanted the attention from everyone that he was still in charge after coming back from solitary confinement. The larger framed man stood up, then looked back down at the man rubbing his sore arm. Cecil raised his large outstretched arms and turned around so all could see who was victorious.

"But the next time you lie or steal from me, I will break that arm of yours off and beat you with it! Do you understand me? Now get your sorry ass out of my sight," promised Cecil, as he looked around to see if anyone else wanted a piece of him. There were no more newcomers, so he sat back down at the table in the middle of the huge room. One of the guards walked over to Cecil and raised his face shield to talk.

"That was a good thing you didn't hurt that guy. I would have hated putting your ass back in the hole, Locklear, and you won't get another chance, so don't screw it up." Cecil looked up and smiled, knowing nothing was going to happen to him. He knew right then his new boss or bosses were more powerful than a few prison guards, but he still didn't know who was actually pulling the strings. He watched as the guards slowly began to disperse as if nothing had happened, and shortly everything in the general population area went right back to so-called normal within a few minutes.

A few hours later three of Cecil's boys came back over to sit down at the same table, but they did not say a word and prayed that he was not in one of his bad moods. But Cecil was feeling pretty confident with the knowledge of his newfound power over the guards, maybe the warden as well. Cecil looked at his small gang knowing what he had in store for them.

"Alright here's the deal you assholes. It looks like I'm getting out of here. When, I don't know. But we need to stick to our plan and remember where and when we are to meet in North Charleston." All three looked at each other not knowing what to say or do. "That's fine boys; I understand I can be a bit hot-headed at times. But for your information I'm OK."

"Yeah, Cecil, I was about to ask if you were alright. We and the rest of the guys were all worried about you in the hole," said Lawrence Wanamaker, known to his friends as Louie. Cecil called him Screwy Louie because he was a real nut case and one sex-crazy nut job. Louie had been charged with all kinds of crimes, one of which was being a pedophile.

Being a pedophile in prison meant that most inmates wouldn't have a thing to do with you. But Cecil took exception, making Louie one of Cecil's most loyal subjects who would do about anything for Cecil. "We all are glad you are out of the hole. It's good to have you back, sir," Louie said, as the others quickly bobbed their heads in agreement. Cecil turned to face the other two.

"Yeah, well I hope you boys feel the same way as Louie, being that I was the one that went to solitary confinement so you two wouldn't get caught."

"No, Cecil we are grateful, without a question we are, thank you so much sir," said one.

"Yes sir, we sure are," with their heads still bobbing in the affirmative. They were scared to death as they turned their heads away in pure shame for their foolish behavior. Cecil leaned over and grabbed a cigarette out of Louie's front shirt pocket. He was noticing and watching how the guards were reacting and knowing that he had his men back under his thumb and was back in charge. Cecil was feeling pretty good about himself as he looked over at a Louie.

"You got a light? Now let's get down to business," he said as the four huddled around the table. Cecil listed his instructions for his new enterprising ideas for making money on the outside. After almost 10 years, counting those three nut jobs, Cecil had amassed an army of loyal subjects of over 57 inmates, along with several of their relatives outside prison, who were already putting his plan in motion. It would be only a matter of time now before one of the largest drug syndicates in the southeast would be starting up and located just outside of Charleston, deep in the swampy marshlands of South Carolina's coastal low country. Cecil knew someone was pulling the strings, but who?

The Question

Chapter 24

THE INTERROGATION ROOM WAS VERY SMALL, hardly large enough to fit two chairs and a table. The two detectives stood hovering over the pretty blonde-haired suspect. Her once perfectly applied makeup was now an intermingling and melting rainbow of all different colors that smeared across her face as she wiped her crocodile tears that were streaming down. Her voice sounded weak, broken, and delicate, as she tried to plead her case to the two detectives, but they weren't buying it.

"How many times do I have to tell you guys? I did not kill my husband. I loved Danny," she sobbed, as one of the detectives handed her a tissue out of a box of Kleenex to stop the bleeding of mascara. "He was everything to me," she said, as the waterworks started to slow and she began to catch her breath, slowly calming down. Detective Matt Baranski grabbed her hand.

"Look, Ms. Gambaro, we are not here to hurt you or make you even more upset than you are with the loss of your husband. But our job here is to find out what exactly happened to your husband and to find his killer. Someone having that much poison in his system didn't get that way from an accidental bee sting. The toxicology report from the boys in the lab said it would have taken four or five million bee stings to add up to that amount of poison found in your husband's body.

"So we're asking for your help, Kimberly, that's all. Now please try hard to remember back to that day or maybe the day before. Was there anything you can think of that seemed odd or out of place, you know, not normal, anything, anything at all? And trust me, after that you are free to go," said Detective Matt Baranski.

"No, I can't think of a thing," she said.

Suddenly the door opened, surprising all three as a police officer appeared in the doorway. "Detectives, this gentleman said he was her attorney," announced officer Rainy, as a very young, but a very sharply dressed young man walked into the already overcrowded room. He was dressed in a $2,000 suit and wearing $600 shoes, along with a million-megawatt smile.

"No, detective, she is leaving now. She is through talking to you gentlemen," said the young attorney with an outstretched hand. "I'm Matthew Cohn, attorney at law." The two detectives did not extend their hands. Cohn quickly turned his attention to his client and handed her another tissue. "Matthew Cohn, at your service Mrs. Gambaro." She grabbed the Kleenex and on clue the waterworks started once more. "Please, we must be going."

"Going? Hell no, sir, she's not going anywhere," shouted Matt. "She is being questioned by Detective Tommy Riddle and me. I'm Detective Baranski and who the hell are you again?"

"I'm so sorry I intruded on your interrogation, gentlemen. And I also know I'm not exactly welcomed here, but again I am Matthew Cohn. I'm here to represent Ms. Gambaro as her attorney. Now, we can all sit back down and go back over your questioning, but I assure you gentlemen, I will stop her before she answers any of your questions. And by the way here's a letter from your very own DA asking for her release."

Baranski was pissed as he shouted, "Who are you again, some hotshot attorney? Well, you see here Mr. Cohn, she will answer, or we will hold her for 24 hours and you can't do one damn thing about that."

The door opened once again and in walked the chief of police. "Baranski, may I have a word with you," as the chief stepped back outside into the hallway and Baranski followed.

"What now?" Baranski said under his breath.

"I heard that, Matt, but you guys are going to have to let her go. I'm sorry but the word came from on high."

"And on whose authority, God's?

"No, in this case, it's your wonderful mayor's."

Baranski could not believe his ears. "The mayor, are you kidding me? Damn boss, what is going on here? This case is getting crazier by the second. I have a suspect who owns a large insurance company here in town to suddenly disappear. A man is found dead in that same insurance agent's office. And now the wife of the dead man is being represented by a million-dollar lawyer she does not even know. And now today, you are telling me to stop the interrogation and just let her walk because the mayor, who usually never gets involved, is now saying to do so? Damn, chief, what's a guy to think?"

"Look, Baranski, just do it. Let the woman go, and I'll buy you a beer tonight, OK?" The chief turned and walked away. Baranski stood and watched as the chief walked back down the long hallway to his office and shut the door.

"Fricking puppet," Baranski uttered under his breath.

"I heard that," shouted the chief from his office.

Baranski turned and walked back into the room. "OK, Ms. Gambaro, I have one more question, then you are free to go."

The attorney turned to his client. "You don't have to answer his questions." She looked back at Baranski.

"OK one question. What is it, detective?" she asked.

"How long was your husband working undercover for the CIA? Or was it the FBI? Which one was it?" Baranski studied her reaction as a surprised look appeared on her face. You could tell she was thinking: how did you know that? But Baranski noticed that she really didn't look that shocked by the question at all.

"You can't be serious," said her attorney, as he stood up and pulled his client up with him. "She is not about to answer that stupid question. Please, Ms. Gambaro it's time we leave."

Matt and Tommy watched as the two slid around the table and left the small interrogation room. They shut the door, leaving the two detectives still standing inside. "What was that question all about, Matt? That came out of left field."

"Sometimes it's not what you ask, Tommy, but the way they react to the question that counts."

"Did you get what you were looking for?"

"I think so, but we'll see." Baranski then turned as they walked out of the room, flipping off the light switch to the small room as they stepped out.

"Do you really believe this Gambaro character worked with the CIA?" Tommy turned around and asked Matt as they were walking down the hall to their office.

"I don't know, Tommy, but I believe we need to start being detectives and find out. I want you to go over to the Hoover building and I'll go out to Langley. Somebody has got to know something and Tommy boy, you and I are about to find out."

Colombian Smoke Screen

Chapter 25

THE SPEEDING RED CORVETTE CONVERTIBLE maneuvered as if it were on a giant slalom course cutting its way through the fog and slipping around the winding coastal roads overlooking the waters of the Chesapeake Bay near Annapolis. Jack drove Connie almost to the airport saying hardly a word; both had their minds squarely on the case. Suddenly Connie broke her silence.

"What about Bob's story, the one he told Kay and me about South America and the drug cartels?"

"Yeah right, and I'm Richard Petty," said Jack, as he downshifted the convertible to second gear making the car go faster, pretending to be a racecar driver.

"That's funny, Jack. But really maybe he was telling the truth. What if the government did buy drugs from Colombia and in turn they shipped them through Venezuela to sell back to the United States in an operation conducted by the CIA to win confidence of the Colombian traffickers so the CIA could infiltrate their gangs? It could happen."

Jack had heard enough as he slowed the car down and pulled over on the shoulder of the road, eventually stopping the car. He then turned off the engine and looked squarely at his wife. "It did happen, Connie. At least it tried to happen."

"It did, how do you know this, Jack?"

"The problem was it did not work. It was stopped before it was started because officials were afraid that the US would end-up selling its own drugs back on the streets of Miami courtesy of the US taxpayers. I know it, Connie, because I was one of the guys in Venezuela working with General Ramon Davila. And I didn't see Bob's ass anywhere in sight."

"And why were you there in the first place, Jack?"

"I was a part of a special task force sent by the Army to set up an anti-drug program in major cocaine-producing and trafficking areas of South and Central America, using the country's military, mostly National Guard."

"Why the National Guard?"

"Because, Connie, those guys controlled not only these countries' borders, but the lifeline for any drug dealer, the highways."

"How do you know it didn't work?"

"Will you let me finish!" Connie sat back in her seat waiting for his answer. "The proposal was to allow hundreds of pounds of pure cocaine from Colombia to be shipped to the US through Venezuela working with the anti-guerrilla forces in El Salvador. And yes, the mission was to infiltrate the Colombian gangs and win their confidence. The idea was to gather as much intel as possible on the drug gangs themselves, but as far as I know, the plan never took place. Later that year I was sent to Iraq."

"So what you are saying is it could have happened. Sweetheart, you were not there, so in truth how would you know for sure?"

"Yeah, I guess you're right, sure, but I think I would have known something about it. I think I would have heard something from one of my men. They would have known something I believe, and I had some of my best men there. You know most of them, like "Oilcan" Phil Owens, "Recoil" Remick, and "Rain Man" Ray Putnam. Heck you saw Steve Hyatt's coffin at Andrew's, and of course, Rhys, he was there as well."

Connie stopped listening as Jack continued to talk. Her face felt numb. She could not believe what she was hearing. How did she miss that? It was so simple, the answer to all the murders was right there in front of them the whole time. She looked back at her husband.

"Shut up, Jack!" she shouted. "Listen, don't you see, the story is true. The men in your outfit, all of them dead accept you and Rhys. All of them were out of your outfit, Jack, all that were sent to South America."

"Their deaths were all considered accidents or killed in action, Connie. They are all closed and shut cases."

"Sure they are, but what if they weren't accidents? What if someone in the CIA was killing off every one of your men to keep the operation quiet? What if that was the case Jack, and if so you and Rhys would be next, right?"

"I don't know, Connie. That seems a little farfetched. I can't think of anything about that mission that would cause someone to kill me and my men."

"No, but maybe they don't know that, Jack. Maybe we just stumbled into it, but they don't know that. Think back, is there something you could have missed about the mission? Think hard, Jack."

Jack sat looking over the hood of his car and down the road as his mind's eye was seeing the faces of his men just as clear as day. He knew what she was saying made a lot of sense as he started looking back at the situation, but why would anyone want to kill off his whole unit? It didn't make sense, but he wasn't about to rest till he found out

"Damn, Connie, you might be right," he admitted.

And all these years. Cecil Locklear may have had something to do with it. Jack suddenly turned the ignition switch back on as the Corvette roared back to life.

"Connie, get that car phone out of the glove box and call Kay and Rhys. Tell them that our plans have changed; we'll see them later tonight around 6 o'clock, not this morning. This morning you and I are going to Baltimore to see our friends Bob and his lovely wife Nancy."

Jack quickly spun the little red sports car around on a dime, causing rocks, dirt and gravel to fly as the car ran off the shoulder of the road, then back onto the asphalt as the tires barked with traction.

"Now you're driving like Richard Petty," said Connie as they started to head in a different direction.

Wanting Answers

Chapter 26

CONNIE CALLED AHEAD TO TELL BOB of their arrival. It was around 11:30 am when the red Corvette pulled along the curb in the alley between the old warehouses and what was left of a few row homes that were still standing in the old dilapidated neighborhood. Both Jack and Connie exited the vehicle and approached the rusty metal but solid door with no number or name to be seen on it, and Jack began to unlock the door using the keypad mounted on the wall.

"What?" said Jack. "It's my home. I remember the combination, so what?" He then pressed a small speaker button and spoke.

"Hey Bob, its Jack and Connie. We are coming in." There was no answer. He looked at Connie. "He knew we were coming, right?" Connie didn't say a word but only shook her head in the affirmative, and once again Jack pressed the button and acknowledged they were entering the house.

Still no answer as Jack removed his Smith and Wesson .45 from his waistband and proceeded inside the safehouse with Connie in tow. They stepped in and Jack placed his thumb on the scanner as a laser scanned his fingerprints, which caused the second steel door to open. The Womacks entered the dwelling cautiously as Jack shouted out Bob's name. Suddenly they heard voices coming from upstairs. Responding to the voices they moved in that direction. In a flash Bob and Nancy came out from the bedroom upstairs.

"Sorry, folks, we were busy doing a few things," as it was obvious what they were up to as they quickly straightened and rearranged their clothes. "Really, Jack, you need to put some doors in this place."

Connie started to laugh as Jack placed his weapon back behind his shirt.

"I see you kids still like each other. Hello, Bob, it's good to see you. It's been a long time, you too, Nancy. Sorry about this situation. I didn't mean to barge in on you two. I hope everything with the house is OK." The two shook hands as the Wessons came down the stairs and all four said their hellos. Connie and Nancy sat on the couch while Bob and Jack sat in the two chairs that faced each other near the coffee table.

"So I guess and hope you are here to take us home, right Jack?" said Bob as he looked over at Nancy.

"No, Bob, not at this time. But soon, we hope, real soon. I'm afraid today we are here to ask you a few more questions."

"Yeah, Bob," said Connie, "this whole story about the Venezuelans and the Colombians."

"Yes, Bob please, I need to hear your side of the story to better understand why we, Connie and myself, were involved in the first place," said Jack.

Bob sat there not knowing what to say as he nervously rubbed his hand across his face and pushed his chair back from Jack a little. "Well, OK Connie, Jack, here's what I know. And by the way, Jack, I knew that you and your unit were there as well but I had nothing to do with that."

"You had nothing to do with what, Bob?"

"Dealing with the Venezuelan government, that's why the Company wanted you and your guys. Plus they don't care much for the military; especially when they are trying to hide something, plus the military slows them down and hampers their operations."

"Hamper hell, there wouldn't be any operation half the time if it wasn't for us, and you know it," Jack replied.

Connie looked at her husband. "Jack, let him talk please!"

"Where was I? Oh yeah, the Colombia drug cartel operation, it did occur, and after Connie told us about your men, Sam and I believed that some of your men were so-called accidentally killed to keep the operation quiet. The only reason you were allowed there in the first place, Jack, was to help open communication. You see, Connie, the Venezuelan National Guard and the rest of their military basically run their government. And Jack, after you and your men made sure that was accomplished, your job was pretty much over as far as the CIA was concerned."

"You mean they were expendable," said Connie as she walked around Bob's chair.

"Look, like you say Jack, I didn't call the shots, I just take orders. My orders were to make sure the drugs entered the US port of Miami, that's all."

"No, Bob, my men are dead and this drug thing doesn't add up. Why were they killed, Bob? Who gave that order? That's what I want to know."

"I don't know if your men were killed are not. I was nothing but a soldier just like you."

"We were supposed to be on the same team, Bob," shouted Jack as he quickly stood up and walked away from Bob and looked over at Connie. She immediately stood up and took Jack's place.

"Bob, Sam is dead, all of Jack's men were killed off and now you are in hiding. Jack and I believe you know something or somebody who is behind this whole thing. Heck you might not even know you know it. But please think back. Who was the person or persons in charge of your operation? We can start there."

"The ranking officer was Marc Mc Flanagan, and his attaché in Venezuela was a lady name Abigail Gourley. It was Gail who proposed the shipment. And yeah, there was a little French fella. I don't know his name. He never talked much. But I'm telling you guys there was over 1,000 pounds of the stuff, pure cocaine. It was shipped straight to the United States through Venezuela. And that did happen, and you, Jack, should have known about it because my friend, your men loaded it aboard your C-130 transport that took you boys back home to the District 7 Coast Guard Base which is in Miami, Florida."

"No way, Bob, I was there and I didn't see any of my men carry anything on or off that plane."

"No, Jack, they drove it on. It was in the trucks your men were driving, more than 1,000 pounds of the stuff on your plane by my calculations. The reason I know is because of Danny, you know the dead guy in my office. He and I also helped to deliver it to the FBI and DEA agents in downtown Miami. By the way those six agents are not with us any longer either."

"What, they just vanished?" questioned Connie.

"You could say that, looks like a lot of that was going on," said Bob, as he too stood up and walked over to Jack. "I don't know who is doing this, Jack, but they must be very powerful and insulated. We are talking high levels in the government and maybe military as well. I don't know for sure. All I know is that they were after Danny and now he is gone, and I know I'll most likely be next. And I would watch myself if I were you, Jack."

"And Sam Hornaday knew all of this I Spy stuff that took place as well?" asked Jack.

"Yeah, he knew some but to what extent I really don't know. Hell, I didn't know for sure that your men in your unit had been killed. But I do know that those two detectives that questioned me, Baranski and Riddle, they have been poking around and asking questions at both agencies." Jack sat there with a puzzled look on his face.

"You said Sam knew some but he didn't know everything. What the heck else is there, Bob," replied Connie, as Bob turned his attention back towards the table to face her.

"I'm afraid, Connie, the mission has not stopped. It never has."

"What, it's still going on?"

"Yes, I'm sure of it, and I'm afraid more people are going to die." Jack and Connie could not believe their ears, as Bob continued. "No, the drugs have not stopped, in fact they have intensified the operation altogether. From what I and my partner Danny had gathered there are several more countries now involved, including Iraq, Syria, Iran, maybe even North Korea, and it doesn't seem to be stopping anytime soon. And it is all fully funded by US tax payers. That's why people are still dying, Connie. And I'm afraid no one can stop it at this point."

"So they are using the drugs as leverage to appease and communicate with communist regimes, dictators, and terrorist groups. Well that's great, how screwed up is that!" Connie answered.

"And it's all started by bribing local government officials, who pay off their cops using blood money to boot," said Bob.

"Local cops," said Jack as he sat back on the couch. Suddenly he stood up and looked over at Connie. "OK then, that does it for me. Connie, we need to go. Bob, is there anything you or Nancy need before we go, groceries, money, anything at all?"

Connie was surprised at Jack's sudden need to leave. "Jack, are you alright?"

"Yes, dear, I'm fine. Are you ready, we need to go now," he said nervously.

Not knowing what was going on, Bob had nothing to say as he looked over at Nancy. "No, Jack, I believe we are fine but thank you. We have everything we need. But why are you two having to leave so soon, you just got here?" said Nancy.

Connie grabbed Jack's hand as she turned towards the Wessons. "I know Jack and I'm sure he wants to get started on this as soon as possible. Please call us if you think of anything you need."

"Bob, Nancy, have your bags packed and be ready to move. The next time Connie and I come back here you guys will be leaving and it might be out of the country," said Jack, as he and Connie headed for the door. "Sorry to be so abrupt Bob, but if these folks have eyes everywhere like you say I myself might have compromised your position by just being here."

"I understand," said Bob.

"Well, I don't understand at all," said Nancy.

"I mean we need to get you out of here as soon as possible before the bad guys show up." Jack walked over and kissed her on the cheek and shook Bob's hand goodbye. Connie kissed them both before they exited the apartment. With a tear in Connie's eye she and Jack got in the car and drove off.

Nancy looked at her husband as the Womacks left the safehouse. "Bob why did you tell Jack you didn't know about the deaths of his men? You told me years ago you knew they were all executed."

"Yeah, well, you don't want to tell them everything at once. This way now I'll get Jack and

Connie to really help. Hopefully they will solve this damn thing before all of us are killed."

Tag Team

Chapter 27

THE DC POLICE STATION DETECTIVES' OFFICE was dark in the afterhours of the station and neither detectives Baranski nor Riddle bothered to turn on the lights, which fittingly matched their mood. As they sat in their respective cubicles they pretended to review their notes they had both gathered from their recent investigations of the FBI and the CIA. Both men were afraid of telling each other the truth, knowing full well they came up empty, but before they even had time to sulk the door opened suddenly and the lights came on.

"Yeah, you boys, you always sit in the dark to read?" said Jack Womack as he and Connie walked into the office. The two detectives sat up in their seats and quickly looked up to see who had the balls to barge in their office. Baranski hastily took his feet off the desk as Riddle turned on his desk lamp, as if they had just arrived.

"What the hell are you two doing in here? This office is for police business only. How did you get in here anyway?"

"Tonight Pete's working the front desk," said Connie, as Jack walked closer to Baranski's desk. Both detectives started moving papers around their desk and placing them in folders as if they had something to hide.

"Don't worry Matt, I'm not going to tell anyone that you two came up with zero info with the Feds. Those CIA boys ain't going to tell anybody shit. And neither are the G-men at the FBI, are they, Tommy?" Detective Riddle looked up at Jack, wondering how he knew they had been questioning both agencies.

"How the hell do you know that?" asked Tommy, as he looked back over at his partner.

"Shut up, Tommy, they don't know shit. If they did they wouldn't be here."

"We know about as much as we need to at this point, and a hell of a lot more than you two," Connie said, knowing full well she was lying. But that's what Jack wanted them to think as she played along hoping they would take the bait. Jack quickly pressed Matt even harder.

"If you weren't so damn hardheaded, Matt, I was hoping that maybe if we worked together we could solve this case." Matt looked down at the floor with no response. Jack shouted at his old childhood friend. "Christ, Matt, we grew up together. If not for me, do it for Sam. Hell, Matt, we both would be dead today if it wasn't for the great old man. Sam Hornaday loved us both and you know it."

"I said this office is for official policemen only, not civilians, Mr. and Mrs. Womack!"

"What the hell, Matt, why are you so pissed off at me? I haven't done a damn thing that I know of, so what is it with you?" Matt sat back in his chair and studied the situation, knowing Jack had to need something or he would not be there.

"OK, Jack, what is it?" He then turned to Connie. "What information do you, Connie?" Jack looked over at his wife but didn't say a word. Matt turned his attention back to Jack. "You're right, Jack; we did grow up together in the same neighborhood. Heck, I let you date my sister Lisa. Shoot we were best friends in high school before you stole my girlfriend Keely Braxton."

"Who?"

"You know Keely, Jeff Braxton's little sister, a real cute girl."

"Who the hell is Jeff Braxton?"

"You knew Jeff. We called him Front Butt."

"Front Butt? Why Front Butt?" Connie questioned and Jack answered.

"Because his stomach was so big it had a split in the middle. It really looked like an ass," replied Jack.

"So you do remember?"

"Yeah, but not Keely, I don't remember any girl by that name."

"She went to school with us. She had red hair and green eyes. You don't remember her? You stole her from me. We were in love."

"You have got to be kidding me," said Connie. "You two have been mad at each other for all these years over some girl Jack can't even remember?"

"Bull shit, he remembers, he's just not saying anything in front of you. But that's Jack Womack, always thinking he is better than everyone else, right Jack? Now again, what the hell is it you two want from us?"

"OK, Matt, fine, you win, that's it. I'm sorry you're still mad about some shit that supposedly happened 40 years ago. All I was asking for was some help and a little more time, that's all. Fine, come on Connie let's go!"

"My help? You are kidding me, the one and only Jack Womack is asking for my help! I can't believe it."

"Oh, shut up, I said I'm sorry. Here's the thing. You know I have Bob Wesson and I will be glad to hand him over as soon as I know he is safe."

Matt quickly looked at both Connie and Jack. "You two have had that insurance guy the whole time haven't you? I thought so."

"They did?" shouted Tommy.

"Shut up, Tommy. What do you mean, by you keeping him safe? Hell we're the Washington, DC, Police Department, Jack, and as far as you holding him, last I checked you can't hold our witness. That's called, I believe, obstruction. But go ahead, what else?"

"I need you to get a judge to hear our side and to issue a subpoena on a few CIA agents plus a few other folks and some classified files."

"A judge, really, who Judge Judy? And to subpoena exactly who or what, Jack?"

"Well for starters, basically all US law enforcement agencies. You know the FBI, CIA, DEA, maybe the ATF, and maybe a few of Washington's finest police officers as well. Hell, maybe your department, Matt, also. I don't know but someone needs to pay!"

"Well at least you're not asking for much. Hell, that shouldn't be a problem, but there is one little holdup old friend. You would need literally, an act of Congress." Jack leaned over and put both hands on Matt's desk.

"Not if we have proof of murders," said Connie.

"Several murders, lots of them, Matt, and you don't need Congress for a murder investigation. It's pure unadulterated murder, that's the key that opens about any door in government, and lots of them. And these records I'm asking to be subpoenaed can prove it."

Tommy, being a bystander through the whole thing, finally spoke up. "Murders, who the hell else has been murdered around here?"

"Hold on, Tommy. Now wait a minute, Jack. I appreciate your belief in Tommy's and my abilities. But look here, commander, we are only detectives with the DC police. There isn't a federal judge in this town ready to write a subpoena, summons, or a freaking traffic ticket to arrest folks from the Central Intelligence Agency. Are you kidding me? And if they did you would need a book full of proof, not to mention a few senators and congressmen on board, plus real tangible proof, not just words from a crazy insurance agent like Mr. Wesson. I'm talking hard bona fide evidence, something we can see and touch. Now do you have that soldier boy?"

"I knew coming here was a waste of time, but Connie insisted that I came here first and asked you two before I did it my way."

"Now hold on, Jack, you can't take an army and go up against the CIA and the FBI."

"I don't need an army, Matt, because I was counting on you but don't worry. I'm going to do something, you watch me!" Jack turned to walk out the door when suddenly Matt stopped him.

"Hold it, Jack, wait a minute, maybe we can do something. Hold on," as Matt looked over at Tommy who was sitting with his mouth open.

"Are you crazy? Matt, we are talking the CIA here. Have you two lost your minds?"

Connie and Jack both quickly turned back around as if they already knew that Matt had decided he would help. "OK, Matt, here is what I need you two to do," as she handed him a folder of papers and a list of names starting with Marc Mc Flanagan and his attaché Gail Gourley, plus a few more names of people that Jack and Connie didn't know. "I need some research on these folks."

Matt looked down and read the names. "Are you kidding me, Connie? Do you understand who these people are?"

Connie spoke up. "Yes, we do, Matt. Marc Mc Flanagan is the ranking CIA officer and his attaché. That's why I need you two to dig up a little dirt on those two, something I can use for leverage, you understand, I'm sure."

"Yeah, and I see you threw a few DC cops' names in here too! I'm not a rat, Jack. And what's in it for Tommy and me, jail?"

"How's about one of the largest arrests in the Bureau's history, not a bad collar for a couple of DC detectives, and I'm sure a little money and fame will go along with it. You and I Matt, just like old times, like when we took down the De Angelo gang back in the old neighborhood."

"Yeah, that's what I'm afraid of. This ain't exactly a few pissed off Sicilians we're talking about. No, you want to rain war down on only the United States government here, that's what I'm afraid of."

Connie and Jack walked over to the door to leave. Connie stepped into the hallway first as they both looked back at the two detectives. "It's going to be OK, Matt. We just need a little dirt to get things started," said Jack, as he and Connie walked out of the office. Jack quickly turned back around and looked at Matt again. "But I did save your ass, Matt. That girl Keely you mentioned? She was a sorry piece of ass anyway, plus she's bigger now than her brother Front Butt ever was." Jack started laughing as he and Connie walked out of the detectives' department. As he shut the door he heard Matt shout.

"You go to hell, Womack! You hear me! You go to straight to hell, asshole!"

Jack kept laughing all the way down the hallway. "Baby, you never told me about a girlfriend named Keely Braxton."

"That's because she never was one. But I love messing with Baranski. He is too easy." Jack and Connie kissed and laughed as they walked out to their car and drove off.

Brain-storming Soirée

Chapter 28

CONNIE AND KAY WERE LAUGHING AS THEY walked out of the house to check on the boys. They had exited the kitchen where they were supposedly getting dinner ready, but after a glass of wine or three and a little bit of gossip about Rhys and men in general, they decided to stop acting like housewives and join Jack and Rhys. The two men were sitting on the back deck acting as if they were watching the hamburgers and hotdogs as they smoked their Churchill cigars while Rhys sampled a glass of I.W. Harper, one of Jack's favorite bourbons.

"Hey boys, what's burning?" said Connie with a laugh.

"It's all under control, girls. Rhys has the hose on the ready."

Connie was hoping that this little soirée would help break the ice between Rhys and Kay. Both she and Jack had suspected they were having a fling of romance behind their backs and now was time for it to be out in the open. She watched as Kay walked over and held Rhys's hand.

They all needed a little respite from the case and a get-together for drinks with friends was perfect. After all, by this point the case was going in all different directions, none of which was making any sense. Without anyone saying a word they knew they were all consumed by it. Connie thought that talking about those two having a little romance would at least give them a much-needed break from it all, even though at this stage of the game the case seemed almost impossible to forget.

Nevertheless, every time someone tried to change the conversation, which was mostly Connie, it would eventually circle back to the same reason they were there in the first place, trying to get away from the case. But there was no chance it was going to happen as

Jack looked out over the calming waters of the Chesapeake Bay, with the sound and sights of the Thomas lighthouse flickering in the background.

"You know Rhys, you and I are the only ones from our team that survived after that Venezuela trip a few years back."

Connie looked at Jack. "Please Jack, you said we were not going to talk business tonight, leave the case alone."

But the men just kept on. "No, that's not right, Jack. We all made it back, it's just you and I are the only ones still alive."

Connie spoke up. "And don't forget Rain Man. The authorities have no idea about Ray Putnam. They never found his body."

"She's right, Rhys, and you know as well as I do, he's one pretty tough guy," Jack said as he moved over from one railing to another, all the while looking down into the water.

"Heck, Jack, they were all tough but you can't blame yourself. Those men all died accidently. None were killed in action."

"So you are telling me that four out of five are dead and one is still missing, and it was a fluke, just a terrible twist of fate? Really? Then explain to me how four or five of the greatest soldiers and fighters in the world just happen to die in less than a year apart, all in some freak accident.

"Two were hit by a car, hit and run in both cases. By the way, one was hit by a train. Really, a damn train?" he shouted. "These men had catlike reflexes and you are telling me they got outfoxed by a car and a train. Hell, they said Phil Owens was supposedly shot while cleaning his weapon. Hell, Rhys, Oilcan could clean a nuclear warhead without the thing going off. Accident my ass, they were targets plain and simple."

In a sign of rage he forcefully threw his cigar into the bay below and began to stare deeply into the waters as if he would receive some kind of answer. All three watched for a few seconds, then one by one each walked over to console his boss, their friend, and Connie's husband, but Jack just kept staring as if he was in a trance. Suddenly he broke his silence.

"Baghdad, Al-Few Palace," he said out loud.

Connie looked at her husband. "What about Al-Few Palace, Jack?"

"That's the last mission we all had together," Rhys answered.

Jack looked up from the handrail. "Everything went sideways after that damn mission."

Kay Shirley thought for a second, and then spoke. "Al–Few is that right, the Al-Few Palace? I can't believe you guys are talking about that place. I saw a show on PBS dealing with the Iraq war where they were talking about that place just the other night."

Connie looked over at her girlfriend, "PBS—really? Wow, you truly do need to get out more."

"Yeah well, it was an unsolved mystery, the kind of show I like, talking about where the British army believed they had found some of Hussein's lost millions. It turns out that his fortune was smuggled out of the country right at the beginning of the first Iraq war in thousands of gold brick bars from that palace you were talking about," said Kay.

"Gold bars," said Rhys. "How much are we talking about?"

"Truckloads, and get this, they used tanker trucks. That's right, fuel trucks to be precise, over 10 trucks in two different convoys and, by the way, most of the trucks they found were empty. And get this, no one to this day knows the exact whereabouts of the fortune."

"Jack, do you believe this has to do with our case?" asked Connie.

Rhys could not believe his ears. "Jack, we saw those trucks leaving the palace. I don't know what's going on but this whole damn thing is getting pretty crazy."

Jack then turned and looked at everyone as if he knew something. "Maybe that's it, Rhys." Everyone turned to hear Jack's answer. "Maybe we have solved part of the puzzle. The crazy part was their intentions all along."

"Whoever 'they' are?" asked Kay.

Connie looked at Kay. "Whoever 'they' are usually turns out to be big and powerful."

"I'm thinking we're dealing with some kind of underground organization that is both large and powerful and well-connected in all forms of government. To pull this off they would have to be," said Jack.

Rhys chimed in, "Well, it sure as hell can't be the workings of only a few people. Hell, it took an army to get the stuff out."

"And this whole time it's been about stealing gold," said Connie, as she grabbed Jack's arm. "Jack if we are right there no way we can handle this case on our own, and who can we trust?"

"Each other," said Rhys. "That's all we got, Connie."

"He's right, Connie, that's all we got," said Jack as he hugged his wife. "From the beginning with missing gold from Iraq, and to the Colombia drug cartels, the whole thing is intertwined with two or three cases, like the accidental deaths of my men, along with the assassination of Sam Hornaday. Then you add the crazy involvement of Bob Wesson, plus the death of his friend Danny, and the wife with the insurance money. The whole damn thing is wild enough, and then you add the CIA, and the FBI. Damn it's all interlinked together somehow, by somebody."

"Now all we have to do is put the pieces together and make them fit," said Connie. "That's all we have to do. Damn, what a puzzle and who's going to be the next piece?"

"Yeah, and doing it without getting killed in the process, now that's the trick," said Jack as all nodded their heads in agreement.

Lost And Almost Found

Chapter 29

THE ONE-EYED MAN WITH A LARGE SCAR across his face drank by himself in the back corner of an old South American bar. The cantina looked much like a scene from some old John Wayne western. Every time the wind whistled through the old adobe building the dirt and stench blew in like it did in so many old bars in the rough side of a rough town.

No one seemed to know much about the one-eyed man or where he came from and many didn't dare ask.

Most assumed he was an American but like a lot of people hiding from somewhere or somebody he didn't talk very much, if any. They called him un hombre enojado, which translates to "one mad man."

His nickname fit his reputation of being easily provoked. He often broke out into an unstoppable rage, which led him to win numerous bar fights or brawls. Basically out of pure fear everyone left him alone. It was easier and safer that way. Outcast and feared, he reached over and grabbed the half empty bottle of tequila and washed down the last bite of corn tortilla and beans.

The few customers in the bar watched as he slowly stood. He scanned the room with his one good eye, and then walked over to retrieve the broom that was leaning against the wall in the other corner. He started back to work to pay for his meal. He saw a 3 cent bolívar on the floor and bent over and placed the coin in his dirty pants pocket as he began to sweep the sand and dirt off the floors and out the door.

Everyone seemed to go back to their business as he worked. In the meantime he tried to think back to how he got into this situation. He did not remember how he got there exactly or how he lost his eye, in a fight he guessed. The Special Forces tattoo on his arm reminded him that at one time he lived an extraordinary life, but that memory was also a blank in his very short and selective memory.

The one exceptional feeling he did get was when he was fighting. The scars on his body were proof that his short temper put him in that predicament often. But the feeling he got was an out-of-body experience, as his body took over and his movement was without any conscious thought. It was as if his brain switched off and he went on auto pilot as he became a mere spectator watching his opponents' bodies appear to easily fall to the ground.

His arms and legs turned into dangerous weapons as they punched, twisted, and kicked his opponent into an unconscious state. His reputation was like that of a gun fighter where competition is endless. The money from his winning filled only the pockets of gamblers and bar owners, not his, for his mental capacity left him with only a roof over his head and a few free meals. Being a survivor of blunt force trauma had left him to endure this mysterious life as he tried to deal with countless seizures, blackouts, poverty, and the never-ending pain of migraine headaches. He hoped one day his memory would return and he would be able to leave this self-made prison, but for now he swept.

Once again the doors opened from the outside as two more thirsty strangers entered the nearly empty Venezuelan saloon and took their seats. "Dos whiskeys," one of the men shouted. They were both dressed in military apparel. The one-eyed man stared at the two soldiers. Suddenly he saw a vision. There was something about those two that caused his mind to think back as he tried to reach for answers. But why now, and what was it about these two soldiers, when there had been hundreds of soldiers coming into the cantina before? Why these two? He quickly studied their faces.

"Que demonios est'as mirando?" (*What the hell are you looking at),* one soldier shouted. A few more seconds of study went by and suddenly his brain was on fire with flashbacks and memories. His eye opened wide as his mind started to see horrifying visions that raced through his brain. He could see himself surrounded by soldiers as they repeatedly whipped, hit, and beat him as he lay tied up on the ground. They stomped and kicked him like a dog, as he tried to endure the beating till the pain was too intense. Quickly his vision vanished. His heart was now pounding as sweat covered his face. It was hard for him to breathe. He turned around from the two soldiers to catch his breath.

"Qu'e demonios te pasa?" (What the hell is wrong with you?), the soldier shouted and pointed at him. The one-eyed man got up and quietly walked out of the bar, wiping away tears.

All the locals were now in shock. They had never before seen him with that look of being afraid or even worried. The local patriots at the bar started to talk among themselves about what they had just seen.

"Est'a llorando," (He's crying), one said.

"Nunca lo hab'ia visto atemorizado antes," (I've never seen him scared before), another spoke.

The crowd could not believe what they had seen; here was one of the toughest, most brutal fighters they had ever seen, apparently scared out of the room by only two soldiers and for what?

No one seemed to have a clue as to what had just happened, especially the two soldiers. Without warning the door flew back open. Un Hombre Enojado came charging towards the two soldiers like a bull, knocking both of them and the table over to the ground. Like an unrelenting avenger he began to unleash his fury. He hit one, then the other. With blow after blow from his powerful fists he beat the two soldiers unconscious.

He stopped and rested a few seconds, but he was not at all finished. He then picked one soldier up and threw him down using the man's own weight as a weapon. One by one and repeatedly, he threw each one hard to the ground. You could hear their skulls crack as their bodies hit the floor with a hard thud.

The one-eyed man's arms tired so he started kicking them till he could kick no longer. After several minutes the carnage finally ended as he stopped and caught his breath. The heap of flesh and bone was unrecognizable. He stumbled over to a table and collapsed on a bar stool as he looked around the room. No one said a word as they tried to understand what had just happened. He himself was not completely sure. Was it out of rage or revenge? His mind again went blank, the gruesome beating and flashback of his memory over.

Soon word of the killing got out and within minutes whistles and police sirens filled the air.

Showing no sign of an urge to run from capture, the one-eyed man sat and waited. The police arrived but out of fear they too waited in hopes of reinforcements of more soldiers. Eventually more men came and surrounded the small bar. Several minutes ticked by till finally the word was given. The large force of soldiers and policemen stormed into the small bar with their guns drawn, but there was no resistance.

They easily manhandled the one-eyed man off the stool and pulled him up across the bar as they forcibly applied handcuffs to his large wrists. They then forced him up and directed him out of the door and finally placed him in the police car. The locals stared into the vehicle and noticed the look of shame on his face. Not once did he try to stop them or put up any kind of fight. They watched the car drive off down the dusty street and to the police station.

Surprise Caller

Chapter 30

THE HOUSE WAS QUIET AS JACK TYPED ON HIS COMPUTER: I need the following men to assemble at our Maryland office at 0900 hours, on the 15th and be ready to travel south of the equator. I need Garret-Rountree-Stone-and Mason. If there are any conflicts, please advise Rhys Garret or me ASAP.

Suddenly Connie spoke as she watched Jack working on his computer. She was wondering why the house was so quiet. The two had hardly talked to each other since last night at the little get-together with Rhys and Kay. Their thoughts from last night's conversations were still marinating in their brains. "Is everything alright babe? What are you doing in the dark, you trying to act like Matt and Tommy at the police station?" as she tried to laugh and he did not.

"No, I was just sending a message to my men. He turned and looked at Connie. "It's time I do something, that's all," he replied.

She leaned over his shoulder and read his message and read the last part out loud. "Be ready to travel south of the equator. No, Jack, you don't need to go down there. You heard what Bob said, that mission is still active. Let's say everyone in your outfit was killed but you and Rhys. That doesn't mean you have to solve it. Don't push your luck, Jack. You need to let the military handle it, not you!"

"I heard you, Connie, but I can't just sit here and not do anything when I still have one man missing." Jack pressed the send button on his computer, sending the message by email to his men. "I won't sit here, Connie. I'm going to at least try to do something about it. Ray Putnam deserves at least that much. You wouldn't want them to just forget about me, now would you?"

"No, but don't you think you need to call someone, maybe like someone at the Pentagon first?" Suddenly the phone began to ring.

"That must be the pentagon calling me back now!" Jack said sarcastically.

"Oh be quiet, smart butt," she laughed as she hit him on the arm, then reached over and picked up the phone receiver from Jack's desk and answered.

"Hello, this is Connie."

"Mrs. Womack, Linwood Massey here with Lloyds, how are you this afternoon? Is this a good time to call?"

"Yes, Mr. Massey, this is fine. I'm sorry I haven't called you back. My husband came home from overseas, and well, it's been a real busy time for us here lately. I'm so sorry to put you on hold like this. I should have called you sooner. Please accept my apologies."

"Now, now, Connie stop apologizing. There's no need to worry. You are fine. Lloyds of London's offer is still on the table anytime you want it. You only need to say the word and the job is still yours, Connie."

"Oh Mr. Massey, thank you so much."

"Please call me Linwood."

"OK, Linwood, thanks again, I would love to join your company. I will need a few days, maybe a couple of weeks or so until the matter at hand is settled. I hope you don't mind."

"No, not at all, but the main reason I was calling was to inform you that we feel that we have discovered some interesting information on the Isabella Stewart Gardner case. You know the case, the theft in the museum in Boston. I believe you were personally familiar with the case."

"Familiar, I have given years of my life trying to solve that caper. And every time I thought I had it, something else popped up and proved me wrong."

"Well, how would you like to get another crack at it? As of right now Lloyds has exclusive rights to the case and I would love to offer you the position as lead investigator. How does that sound?" Jack set back in his chair overhearing the conversation.

"You want me to head up the Isabella Gardner case? Oh, Mr. Massey, I mean Linwood, I don't know what to say," she said as she looked over at Jack for encouragement. Jack, overhearing a part of the conversation, started shaking his head yes, giving Connie his blessing. Then she shouted out a resounding "yes" into the phone receiver. "Yes, Mr. Massey, Linwood, I accept your offer."

"Well that settles it. I will have my secretary follow-up and send you all the pertinent information. I hope you will be able to quickly finish what you are currently working on so we can welcome you aboard, Mrs. Womack. And again welcome to Lloyd's of London." And with that he hung up the phone.

Connie looked down at Jack with a smile from ear to ear. "They want me to head up the investigation on the Gardner case," she said as both Jack and she started to laugh. "Lloyd's of London called me, Jack, how cool is that?"

Jack looked deep into her eyes. He was so proud of his wife. "Everyone wants you, Babe. You are the best, how many times do I have to tell you?"

"As many times as you like," she said as she crawled into his arms. The two embraced and kissed each other for the longest time. However, the mood quickly changed as Jack began to speak.

"That's going to work out great. You'll now be working with Lloyds and I will be off in Venezuela. That's perfect."

Connie quickly pushed him back as she looked up at Jack. "Now wait one minute, mister, no one said you should go down to a who-knows-where third-world country and start your own cartel war with a bunch of crazy drug smugglers. You have no business going down there, Jack. It's not your fight!"

"Not my fight? Those were my men that died, Connie, and after I talk to Admiral Ballantine I believe someone will be going down there real soon and it might as well be me. I have to try to find Ray," he said as he argued his case.

Disgusted, Connie fought to get off his lap and before leaving the room she turned back and gave him a look. That look was one that all husbands know all too well, and one Jack had seen many times before. She walked out of his office forcefully slamming the door with a loud bang. Jack knew she was mad but the mission in this case would have to come first. Suddenly his thoughts were interrupted by the sound of the door bell ringing.

"Someone is at the door," shouted Connie as she was in no mood to answer.

Jack replied under his breath, "Great, don't worry sweetheart I'll get it," as he headed downstairs to the front door. But before Jack could even open the door he heard the sound of a large truck driving off. Sure enough, as he opened the door the brown UPS step-van had already driven off and was halfway down the street.

I can never get to the door fast enough to catch those guys, Jack said to himself as he looked down at the plain brown box sitting on the front stoop. *It must be something for Connie,* he thought, as he picked up the shoebox-sized container and placed it on the kitchen counter. Jack's inspection of the box wasn't very Jack-like. He didn't look at the box very long at all and he never noticed the markings on the box or the lack of them, not even a return address, nothing. But he was in a hurry to get to the office, so after his once-over, he quickly placed it on the kitchen counter and left the house without another thought.

Southern

Welcome

Chapter 31

**THE SPANISH MOSS GREW LONG AND
THICK AS** it hung in the ancient large live oak trees
that paralleled each other lining the driveway like huge
umbrellas to frame the entrance of the once beautiful
and historic plantation. It was a true vision straight out
of the movie *Gone with the Wind,* but the years had been
hard and cruel to the old girl from long years of neglect.
The white paint was now old and faded and the large
mansion itself was badly in need of repairs, at least
that's the way it seemed to the driver of the black SUV
as it pulled up to the large porch in the front of the
home.

A tall, large man stepped out of the car and looked at the familiar landscape before going to the back of the vehicle to remove his luggage from the compartment. He stopped for a second to hear the sounds and watch the waters of the river, just like the one he grew up on in North Carolina. He was very familiar with this river that ran back behind the large house that sat for years along the banks of the Great Pee Dee River. He watched its majestic waters creep downstream knowing its journey was only a few more miles till it reached the Waccamaw River near the city of Georgetown, then into Winyah Bay. From there it would eventually spill out into the great Atlantic Ocean.

He turned to retrieve the bags, but he stopped once again as he closed his eyes and inhaled a large breath of air, smelling the sweet smells of honeysuckle and confederate jasmine on the vine along with his newfound freedom. His memory rushed back to his childhood when his family moved to the waters of Cape Romain and Bulls Bay, not too far from this place at all. His home certainly wasn't a plantation, more like a burned-out trailer, but it was these marshes of the South Carolina low county he loved and missed so much. His dreaming suddenly ceased when the front door opened and a distinguished looking gentleman fitting the description of Colonial Sanders appeared with white hair, beard, and all. He walked out onto the front porch to greet his new guest.

"Welcome back home to South Carolina, Mr. Locklear. I see you are enjoying the sights and sounds of our beautiful river. I'm Godfrey Blankenship, but please call me Freddie, everyone does. I help out here from time to time, kind of make sure things run the way they should if you know what I mean." He spoke with an English accent. "Please come in. You must be tired from your long flight from Kansas, plus the drive from Washington."

"No, I'm not feeling too bad, slept on the plane mostly," he said as he bent over to retrieve his luggage.

"Heavens, please no, don't touch them; I'll get someone to take your bags," as Cecil walked up the steps to meet the man with a handshake.

Suddenly a shy-looking young lady wearing nothing but a night shirt and barefooted, a girl really, came running up to the old man and stopped and stared at the ground. She then spoke. "Yes sir, you called?" She continued staring downward as if she did not dare look up.

"Well hurry up girl and get the bags. Get the gentleman's luggage and be quick about it. And what took you so long?" he shouted. Without hesitation she quickly went over to Cecil and one by one she started wrestling the bags away from him. "And place them in the upstairs drawing room. Tell Thomas we will be having a drink in the bar area later. Now go," he shouted once more.

"Wait, young lady. I'll help you," said Cecil as he offered to help with his luggage.

"No, I won't hear of it. You are my guest." Cecil stopped and the two watched as the young lady struggled up the steps. The small girl could hardly manage to pick the bags up as she struggled with them all the way into the house.

"It's so hard to get good help these days, isn't that right, Mr. Locklear?"

"Please call me Cecil, and yeah I guess so, but it's been a while since I did any real work, other than making license plates," he laughed. The laugher was not returned, as Freddie motioned for the two to enter the house. Cecil followed him inside.

The house was dark and grey and completely empty. Its walls were totally bare. It was truly a dump. There was hardly any furniture, and what furnishing there was, was not worth keeping. The floors were filthy with no carpets or rugs of any kind on the floor, just dust and broken plaster. The walls had holes in them but no pictures or paintings and the windows were blacked out.

A couple of oil lamps lit the areas where there was no sunlight. The exterior, Cecil thought, was bad but this was straight out of the Addams Family. It was a plantation from hell he thought. Freddie walked over to a large panel door and placed a key inside a small box. Suddenly a door opened to an elevator. The two entered the elevator and it swiftly descended several floors and then stopped. The doors opened as Freddie pointed to Cecil.

"Please, after you, Mr. Cecil," as the two walked out of the lift into a massive room, this time well lit.

"Wow, now this ain't bad," said Cecil as he walked into the large open room with all the amenities one would ever want. Dozens of large-screen TVs lined the walls in every room. A full wet bar that circled half the room was filled with every kind of liquor one could imagine. Great looking furniture, all leather, along with poker tables, pool tables, and dart boards in the corners were scattered throughout the area. Oil paintings, real ones by Picasso, Monet, and Gauguin were all over the walls. There was even a stage for entertainment with several rows of seating. This is it, Las Vegas underground, Cecil thought.

"How do you like this, Mr. Cecil? Is this more to your liking than upstairs maybe?"

"Wow," was all he could say at the moment as he walked around looking into each room. There must have been at least 10 bedrooms, all with mirrored ceilings and each with its own bathroom complete with a walk-in shower or tub. There were so many rooms Cecil lost count as he walked back to the main room.

"We call this area the auction room, where all sales are final," laughed Freddie.

"Sales?" Cecil questioned. "What kind of sales are you talking about?"

Freddie walked over and opened a metal door. Behind it were metal bars, a jail cell of sorts. "Human, of course, you didn't think that you were released early from prison to run a daycare, now did you? No, Mr. Cecil, like you were told, we will allow you to run your drug business only if you manage our business as well. Is that totally understood?"

He knew he had no choice, knowing he would never make it out of that bunker alive if he objected to the terms. "No, that's fine. I have just never seen an operation on this scale. It's very impressive, very much indeed," he said as he slowly inspected the compound once again, this time more thoroughly. "How many girls and how often?" he asked.

"There are not only girls going through here and as far as schedules, trust me, Mr. Cecil, you will be notified. Now you do understand this is not your house to live in. You will need to make your own arrangement shortly. We only use this for special guests on special occasions, understood?"

Cecil was having a hard time being told what to do and had had about enough of it. "You keep asking if I understand, Freddie, and I keep telling you I understand, OK!" Cecil shouted.

Freddie looked Cecil dead in the eyes. "My job is to manage, because Mr. Cecil, if you do not comply, there will be no question about your fate. Now is that completely understood?" There was a moment of silence. Then Freddie patted Cecil hard on the back in an effort to ease the tension. A ding sounded as the elevator once again opened. Cecil could not believe his eyes as his old army buddy walked out of the elevator, Thomas Wise, better known to Cecil as Skeeter. They had not seen each other in several years, but strangely Skeeter walked by Cecil without even acknowledging that Cecil was present. He walked over and stood in front of Freddie without saying a word.

"Good timing, Thomas. I'm sure you two would like to talk about old times but first please make us a drink." Without hesitation and without a hello Skeeter walked straight behind the bar and started to work. It was as if he was under some kind of spell. "Now what do you think about your old friend, Mr. Cecil, not the chatter box he once was?"

"I don't how you did it; hell, I've tried to shut him up for years!" Cecil and Freddie started laughing. The only one not laughing was Skeeter, as he placed ice in the two glasses.

"You see, Mr. Cecil, even a best friend can be turned in a way to be more reasonable. It's imperative with our clientele that our product is of the highest quality and must be kept under control so as not to be damaged. Using strong narcotics to control or sedate can only be used as a last resort. We want them to be able to perform when delivered.

"This is the reason why you are here, Mr. Cecil. We needed someone with your military background in psychological warfare and your ability dealing with extreme interrogation techniques. Now let's make a toast," as the two men raised their glasses in the air. "To our new enterprising venture."

"Here, here," shouted Cecil, "to our new venture!"

Venezuelan Visitors

Chapter 32

JACK GOT OUT OF HIS CAR AFTER ARRIVING AT his airfield office on the other side of a long row of airplane hangars. He watched as a plane took off and stared as it vanished out of sight. The weather was perfect, a beautiful day, not a cloud in the sky. What a great day to fly, but not today. He knew it was not going to happen today, not when duty calls, he thought, as he walked closer to his building. But this is the life of a business owner, work never seems to stop, he thought, and he was right. Suddenly the door to his office flew open with Rhys standing in middle of the doorway and calling for Jack.

"Jack, hurry up and come inside. You have an important call from Southern Command," shouted Rhys as he darted back into the building. Jack picked up his pace and hurriedly entered the line shack just off the runway.

"What the hell, Rhys, what is it?" He then stopped talking as the voice on the radio was piped over the loudspeakers so Jack could hear over the static and cracking sounds.

"He is here now, lieutenant commander, please repeat your statement again, over," Rhys requested as he keyed his microphone.

"Roger that, Rhys. I said it seems one of your MIAs has been found, Jack. We found him down here in South America. It doesn't look good at all, Jack. Like I said, he appears to be one of your soldiers. He is in jail awaiting trial, over." Jack looked at the speaker as if the man was standing right there in the room.

"Roger that. Wait a minute, Harry. Harry Wagner is that you, over?" Jack thought it was Lieutenant Commander Harry Wagner, the assistant to the commander of the US Naval Forces Southern Command in the 4th Fleet, which was led by Rear Admiral George Ballantine.

"Roger that, Jack, I believe we found your man. Putnam, or at least someone fitting his description. He definitely appears to be military, if only by his tattoos.

He was placed in jail last month. He really should be in a hospital I'm afraid, over."

"Roger that, are you sure it's Putnam? Raymond Putnam? He's in jail for what? How bad is he hurt, over?"

Rhys and Jack stood waiting to hear more as the sounds of cracking static came over the airwaves and then they heard the word.

"**Murder.** Jack, they are holding him on the charge of murder. He supposedly killed two Venezuelan soldiers in cold blood in a bar fight near the town of Cabimas. It's a city on the shores of Lake Maracaibo in Zulia State, over."

"Murder charges? Over." Jack shouted.

"Roger that, plus he has serious mental problems, Jack. He won't talk to anyone down here. Maybe he'll talk to you or one of your team members. I just wanted to give you a heads-up first before the news broke in the states. I'll call you back when I get more info and at least a better cell signal, over."

"Roger that, Harry, please do. I need more info ASAP, over."

"Roger that, Jack, this is So Com fleet, over and out."

Jack stared at the speaker on the wall as the communication stopped and the line went back to static. Jack and Rhys both looked at one another for a few seconds. Jack sat down in his chair behind his desk and looked up once again at Rhys. "Wow, now that's some shit," said Jack as he placed both hands on the side of his face.

"Man oh man, murder really, there's no way, not our Rain Man," said Rhys. "It can't be him. That's all there is to it."

"I knew he was alive, but damn not like this." Jack stopped and gathered his thoughts for a second or two. "And mental problems too. Hell, I guess it could be so, it's been what, five and a half, maybe six years since he went missing," said Jack as Rhys handed him a cup of coffee.

"I don't know, Jack, lost in the jungle for five or six years, that's a long time. I wouldn't get my hopes up if I were you. That's a lot a body has to endure, probably beaten and tortured every day for five damn years. That's asking a lot for someone to handle."

Jack turned on his computer and started writing an email. To Rountree, Stone, and Mason: Time frame has moved up, be on the ready. We will be mustering at office in 24 hours, headed to Cabimas, Venezuela. He then turned and looked up at Rhys.

"Can you have the plane gassed and ready to launch ASAP? We are leaving tomorrow morning for Cabimas. Get whatever you need and call me if you need anything else. I'm going home to tell Connie and get packed."

"Yes sir, I'll have her ready, commander."

"Rhys, you know if that's one of my men down there, I have to try."

"Yes, I know that sir, hell all your men know that. That's what makes them work so hard for you, commander. You are one of the good guys."

"Oh screw you, Garret, go work on the damn plane," said Jack as he grabbed a few things off his desk on his way out the door. He then turned back around to face Rhys. "Hey Lieutenant, thanks, and how about that, Rain Man, damn it boy, Ray Putnam, after all these years, unbelievable," Jack shouted as he headed to his car.

Rhys just smiled as he shook his head watching his commander drive off. "We are coming Rain Man, we are coming soon!"

Missing

Chapter 33

JACK'S CLOTHES WERE LAID OUT ON THE BED as he folded them neatly into his travel bags. Connie had pleaded her case to go with him.

"Remember I'm the one that can speak Spanish. You don't, so that's it, I'm going with you to find Ray," Connie argued as she watched Jack pack his bags for tomorrow's trip to Venezuela.

"Look sweetheart, I would love for us to go off on a vacation to South America. I have no problem with that. But Babe, this ain't going to be a vacation trip I'm going on. You see these guns I'm putting in this bag," as he placed his favorites, a Smith and Wesson .357 revolver and a Glock .45 caliber automatic. "This is serious business. Someone could get hurt and I'm not risking those chances. It could be you."

Connie knew she was not going but she tried to put up a good fight. After all, Jack and she had made a pact years ago when they first got married that they would keep their business lives separate from their personal ones. And to this point they had, plus it made life a lot easier that way, and again she knew it.

"OK, Mr. Womack, then will you keep that promise? We are taking a vacation when you get back home, you promise."

"That's a deal, Babe, I promise," as Jack tried to sing the song: "I've got two tickets to paradise, won't you pack your bags, we'll leave tonight. I've got two tickets."

"Stop, please stop. I give in; you can go to South America without me. Just stop before you ruin my favorite Eddie Money song for me. You know I love you," she said as she kissed him on the lips and placed her hand over his mouth," as the two smiled and kissed again. "But you better be safe," she said.

They both then said, "I'll be OK dear, I have Tricks the cat to protect me!" That was a running joke between the two for years, because Jack or Connie would say that about every time they left the house whether it was an insurance investigation or a military campaign. The two laughed and kissed again. Suddenly a knock on the door interrupted their banter.

The two turned and saw Matt Baranski standing at the screen door. "Sorry to interrupt you guys but we need to talk. It's about the case of course. May I come in?"

Jack walked over and opened the unlocked screen door. "Matt, please come in. Where's Tommy? Is he with you?"

"No, and that's something else we need to discuss. It has to do with Tommy."

"Come in, Matt," said Connie. "Have a seat," as all three walked over and sat down in the living room. "Can I get you some coffee or something?" she offered.

"No thank you, Connie, I'm fine but there's something going on and I can't put my finger on it."

"What is it, Matt? You can tell us," said Jack.

"OK, you know that night Sam was shot; Tommy and I made the call to investigate the crime scene, right. Well, we did, and we really didn't find a whole lot of evidence, so I went back the next day for two reasons, one to see better in the daylight and two just to see if we missed anything. You know when you get that feeling that there has to be something else maybe. Well, that's the feeling I was getting, so I went back by myself, and sure enough I found a bullet hole in the doorframe. I didn't see it the first time but this time you could see where someone dug a bullet out with a knife or something sharp."

"Are you sure you didn't just miss it the night before?" said Connie.

"No way, that size of a hole was not there the night before, I'm sure of it. I'm convinced someone dug that slug out of the doorframe to hide evidence."

"And you think Tommy did it. Why's that? You two go back a long way." Jack asked.

Matt leaned back in his chair and looked out the window, then back at the Womacks. "He is lying. I just know it. Tommy said he was going home about an hour before I said I was going home that night. So I watched him leave and then I followed him."

"You followed him," Connie repeated.

"Yeah, I know, but something just didn't make sense to me. Tommy wasn't acting like himself that night. I usually have to get onto him for being too anal. He is picky as hell. But that night he was clumsy, like forgetting to wear his gloves till I told him to. He almost stepped in Sam's blood when we got there. Things like that, stuff he normally wouldn't do, stupid stuff like he was trying to screw up the crime scene. And that's just not Tommy Riddle. He is too professional for that."

Jack interrupted. "So you followed him and then what?"

"I saw him talking to some guy, a fairly small person. He didn't come up to Tommy's shoulder, and the odd thing, he was wearing a trench coat."

"A trench coat, in this hot weather, really? What's his name, Detective Columbo?" laughed Jack.

"Look, I'm serious. The two went back to Sam's apartment building. I watched for about 15, maybe 20 minutes, till Tommy and this other guy came back out. They were laughing and all smiles as they shook hands and they both drove off. You know in a sealed crime scene no one is allowed in that area. Heck we had to move people out of their own home for Christ sake."

"How about the cops that were there? Did they see Tommy and trench-coat man messing with anything?" asked Connie.

"Mess with anything? Hell, they told me they hadn't seen anybody that whole night, claimed they didn't see anybody but me that night."

"Somebody is doing a lot of lying, that's all I can say," answered Jack. "That doesn't make any sense, Matt, and why is everyone lying for Tommy anyway?"

"Because maybe they are lying to cover up for the other guy, Mr. trench-coat man," said Connie. "We need to talk to Tommy and find out who that trench-coat guy is."

"Well, you see that's the other reason I'm here. Tommy Riddle is missing."

"Missing, when?"

"Since day before yesterday. I've called his wife and several family members. They haven't seen or heard from him either. He has not been at work or called me. I checked the evidence room and there's no sign of that bullet he dug out of that doorframe either."

"Well, Matt, it looks like you and Connie will have to find Tommy Riddle or Mr. trench-coat man without me. I'm going out of town in the morning to find some of my own loose ends. I should be back in a few days. Till then work with Connie. You two will find something out I'm sure."

"And Mrs. Gambaro, do you know anything about her, you know Kimberly Gambaro, the dead IT guy's wife?

"No, what about her," Connie asked.

"Well, she's missing too. At least she won't answer my calls or her door bell, and apparently her neighbors have not seen her in days," Matt said.

"Maybe she ran off with Tommy," laughed Jack. Matt just shook his head. Then abruptly a buzzing noise was heard as Matt's pager sounded.

"Sorry guys," he said as he pulled out the pager and looked at the phone number. "It's the station. I need to use your phone."

"Sure, it's in the kitchen," replied Connie, "and be careful, the house is a mess."

Matt walked into the kitchen and found the phone on the counter beside brown UPS package. He pushed the small brown box out of the way as he grabbed the phone receiver and dialed the number of the police station to retrieve his message from the watch commander at the precinct.

Matt listened to the message from the police officer; he could not believe what he was hearing as the shocking news was presented to him. He quickly hung up the phone receiver and with a blank expression on his face walked back into the living room and faced his two friends.

"What is it, Matt? Are you OK?" Connie asked.

Matt blurted out the news he had just received. "He's dead. They found Tommy in the Potomac River about 45 minutes ago, no apparent signs of a struggle. They are ruling his death an accident at this point in time. Can you believe that, no way it could be an accident."

"Is there anything we can do to help?" offered Connie.

"No, I don't think so. I'll talk to you two later," Matt said as he walked out the front screen door.

"Matt, do you want us to go with you?" said Connie as they watched their friend leave.

"No, I'm needed to identify the body first and then I will call Debbie, Tommy's wife. I'll call you guys later. Maybe we can grab a beer at the Blue Duck. Tommy always liked that place," he said, as he held back his emotions. They both hugged each other as they watched Matt walk back to his car and drive off. There was nothing to say as Jack shut the door.

Attempt To Rescue

Chapter 34

THE SHINY BLACK HAWKER BEECHCRAFT HORIZON midsize business jet touched down with flaps down and tires barking as puffs of blue smoke marked the landing spot. The once roaring twin turbofan engines quickly dropped to a low roar as brakes were applied causing the plane to sharply decelerate.

Briefly the engines roared once again but then quickly calmed down to a much slower speed as the jet thrust softened. The sound was more a low hum for a few hundred yards, then even softer as the aircraft seemed to be only crawling as it advanced up the taxi way. Instructions from the air traffic control tower were fed into Jack's headset as he turned towards the international gate for private and corporate aircraft in Cabimas, Venezuela.

Still a large city but once a bonanza in the oil business, with a population of over 300,000, Cabimas was located on the eastern shore coast of Lake Maracaibo. Cabimas was still an important part of the oil production business, but with the oil boom and years of prosperity the city now enjoyed revenue from other resources like tourism, which now drew more people and along with it an increase of violent crime.

Jack taxied the sleek black aircraft with the logo DPS Security on the tail section up to the point on the tarmac where he was instructed by the tower to stop and park, so custom agents and local officials could board and inspect the plane before being allowed to proceed further. The turbofan blades wound down with a loud clicking sound as Jack turned off the engines. He and Rhys started their post-flight checklist, making sure everything was in the off position before deplaning.

"Rhys, before custom agents arrive have Spider recheck all our paperwork making sure it's all in order. I don't want to be here all day due to red tape. I would like to get to the jail ASAP, understood?"

"Yes sir, Jack, will do," said Rhys as he removed himself from his co-pilot seat and walked back to check with the men and Spider in particular. Rhys moved out of the cockpit and looked down the row of seats. All he saw were outstretched arms and legs as the team awoke from their slumber.

"Alright men, rise and shine. The eagle has landed. Let's get that stowed gear out and ready to move. Spider, wake your ass up." Sydney Rountree, aka Spider, was their top communications man. He had been on several ops with Rhys and Jack and was a true professional soldier. Spider was a small man, dressed out at about 145 pounds and about five feet nothing, so brawn was not his strong suit. He was the brains of the outfit, smart as a whip and great with radios, computers, and about any kind of communication device there was.

"OK, I'm up already. What is it you big gorilla? Don't you make me get up and whip your ass."

"Yeah right, you little spider monkey, now get up. Boss wants you to check our papers and make sure it's all in order."

"I told you earlier it's done. Jack had me check it before we left. Trust me everything is fine, passports, letters from the state department office, we are good, Rhys."

"He said check it," said Rhys, knowing full well it was done but just following orders from Jack like always.

"Yeah sure, Garret, you got it," as Spider looked down at the file full of documents and never opened it. "Looks good to me, soldier," as he leaned back in his seat and closed his eyes.

"I said get up," shouted Rhys without looking back knowing Spider all too well.

"Alright all ready," said Spider as he hustled up, grabbing his things from under the seat.

"It's cool little man. He is just doing his job," said DJ Mason, one of the newer members of Jack's team.

"Nice meeting you too, Muscles," said Spider as he quickly left his seat and headed to the back of the plane to check his equipment as a jeep full of Venezuelan and US officials pulled up beside the aircraft. Jack got out of his seat to meet them as the door to the aircraft opened.

The Venezuelan diplomats were first to greet Jack. "Good morning, senor. May we see your papers please?" Jack motioned to Spider who handed over their documents. The large overweight man with a big black mustache snarled and made grunting noises as he read them over, then read them over again. Jack looked over at Spider who looked surprised. After a few minutes the gentleman handed the papers back. "Gracias, Senor, everything appears to be in order," as he handed the papers to Jack and stepped out of the small plane.

"Well, how's it going, Jack? Glad to see you boys made it down to this lovely spot of the world," said

Lieutenant Commander Harry Wagner of the US Navy's southern command.

"Hey, Harry, long time no see, old buddy," as the two shook hands.

Harry removed his sunglasses as he walked into the plane. "Well, Jack, it looks like they will only allow you to see the prisoner, no one else out of your group, just you. You are lucky. It's been one pain in the ass working with these folks let me tell you."

"I imagine they are still pretty pissed off at him after killing two of their own," said Jack.

"Well, that's the deal alright, and they have moved the trial up to tomorrow, so we don't have much time. Are you ready to go?"

Jack looked at Rhys. "Get the men to the hotel in town. I'll meet you back there after I see Ray."

"Yes sir, you got it, Jack, and tell Ray we are all thinking about him."

"Roger that," said Jack as he left the aircraft and got into the jeep and drove off to the other side of the airport. Once there he was greeted by a Venezuelan military official, Lieutenant Perez, plus the US State Department official Candace Martin. Harry introduced Jack to everyone as they climbed into a large black SUV and headed out of the airport parking.

The jail house was on the east side of town about 20 miles from the airport and right in the middle of the worst part of town. They traveled on several major highways, but once they got off the larger interstate-type highways the trip was nothing but third-world. The SUV started cutting in and out of small narrow dirt roads and streets that made you think you were in an American 19th century old-western cow town. Trying to keep from getting car sick, they focused their minds on their final destination. About 45 minutes later they finally arrived.

The SUV came to a stop and pulled up to the large brownstone building with the word C'arcel, meaning jail, on the outside. The four visitors got out of the vehicle. Candace Martin appeared to be straight out of college. She was the assistant to the US ambassador of Venezuela, so she must be smart, Jack thought, looking over at Harry as they got out.

"Whose idea was it to bring this young lady to a prison? I don't think that's a real good idea, do you, Harry?" asked Jack.

"I heard that, Mr. Womack" as Candace took offense to his statement. "I can handle myself just fine, thank you. You know women can do just about anything a man can do, Mr. Womack," she said, knowing this was the first time she had ever been inside a jail house before, and certainly not one in South America.

"I know, I've got a woman just like you at home. Sorry, I was thinking of only your safety young lady," replied Jack as he looked back at Harry. The two just shrugged their shoulders and walked inside the dirty building. The four walked up to the large desk where a policeman sat eating a sandwich. Lt. Perez walked up and started talking to the policeman in Spanish. The rest in the party assumed he was asking to have the prisoner ready so they could talk to him. Suddenly the two broke out in laughter looking over at the three Americans.

Harry looked back at Jack. "That always makes me feel good when they laugh at you."

"Yeah, I feel the love," Jack answered.

Perez looked over to the group. "He said it will be a few minutes, so please follow me to the visitation area." The three followed him a few yards down the hallway. Jack and the rest could hear the sound of the prisoners in the jail getting louder as if they knew a girl was on the way. Another policeman came out of his office to escort the party to the jail.

"Please senors and senorita follow me," he said in English. "Please senorita don't get too close to the prisoners, please I ask you," he warned as they followed him farther down the hall, then out into a courtyard where they saw a small walking track worn down into the ground and row after rows of bar windows. The policeman led them to another door and back into the jail with hundreds of men and boys standing in their cells. The sound of shouts and whistles and jeers were deafening as the female was sighted.

"Please quickly move over this way," said the policeman as he placed his arm around Candace as if he was trying to shield her from the outstretched arms of the prisoners. At the same time the policeman was trying to move the whole group faster and out of the general population area.

Once they passed through a large set of green doors they entered into a large room full of tables and chairs where another group of policemen stood. This must be their version of a visitors' center, Jack thought, as his eyes quickly scanned the area where he noticed a man sitting in the very back of the room. He appeared to be a very large man with a beard from what Jack could tell from that distance. But something was wrong. Jack noticed that the man appeared to be slumped over a table.

"We are here to see the prisoner," Lieutenant Commander Harry Wagner stated.

"Yes, we all know that, senor. That's why he is in here. You have only a few minutes. Please have a seat." The policeman pointed to the four chairs up in front of the room about 20 feet away from the man they came to see.

"I'm sorry, but that's too far away," answered Jack.

"Really, senor, we will need to sit closer so we can see and hear him better," Candace argued.

"Lady, you don't tell me what to do, now sit," he shouted. In response they all did. They sat and watched for what seemed like a few minutes and still no movement of any kind.

"Sir, are you able to hear me? I'm Lieutenant Commander Harry Wagner of the United States Navy. Can you hear and do you understand me? We are here to help you. Are you hurt, sir?"

They still could not see his face and there was no response out of the man. Then Candace said she'd give it a try. "Hello sir, my name is Candace Martin. I work for—" Suddenly his head moved, then his shoulders.

"Keep talking," Jack ordered, after seeing the reaction at hearing a female voice.

"I'm from the state department, Mr. Putnam. I work for the US Embassy here in Venezuela. Can you understand what I'm saying?" The man's movement stopped. However, his head was still down where no one could see his face.

"Soldier, look up here. Damn you, soldier, I order you to look at me," shouted Jack. The man rounded his shoulders as he faced the group, but he was still too far away for anyone to recognize him. "The hell with this shit." Jack had had enough and was tired of being restrained. He got up from his chair and headed toward the prisoner.

"Senor, please back in your seat," ordered the policeman.

"Senor, I said stop, you can't go to him," another shouted. Jack didn't hesitate in his advancement knocking row after row of chairs out of his way and heading in a straight line to his target.

Even shouts of "stop Jack" from the group members failed to deter him. The sound of guns being locked and cocked into firing positions were heard as Jack continued to advance. Jack was almost there when one of the policemen grabbed his arm and placed a pistol to his head, but Jack Womack was not going to be denied as he pushed off his assailant. He finally made it to Ray as he grabbed his friend up by the shoulders and lifted him up so everyone could see his face, and the whole room went silent as they watched.

The expression on Jack's face went blank as well. He suddenly realized that the man sitting in the chair, the man they all came to interview and hopefully rescue, was not Petty Officer First Class Ray Putnam. This was a person only Candace Martin knew as a missing American, a person of interest for years. An escaped convict from Wilcox, Arizona, Warren Blalock was an ex-Vietnam era marine and well-known bank robber and con man. He had been beaten to a pulp. His face was one big mess full of blue swollen bruises and lacerations all over his face and body. Jack felt sympathy for the man as he looked over at the guards and shouted at them.

"This man needs help! My God, he's been beaten damn near to death. What the hell is wrong with you people?" Several policemen walked over and grabbed Jack. "Get your damn hands off me you sons of bitches," Jack shouted, as he was being manhandled and overpowered. He kept shouting as they pulled him away from the prisoner and threw him to the ground. Jack looked back over at the prisoner. A look of thank you was on the man's face as he slumped back into his chair with his head facing downward once again.

"I demand you stop. This is not the way Venezuelans treat our guests yet alone our prisoners," shouted Lieutenant Perez. I want to speak to your Chief of Police Hernandez," he shouted once again. With that the guards released Jack, and the other two of the group went over and joined Jack as they all checked on the prisoner. Perez was on a mission as he walked out of the room and down the hallway in search of the chief with a reluctant guard in tow. The rest of the group attended and huddled around the prisoner, as Harry and Jack inspected his wounds and his overall condition.

"Is it too much to ask if we can please get this man some damn water?" Jack asked. One of the guards quickly handed Jack a bottle of water. Jack first poured some water into his hand to help the prisoner drink. A soft thank you came out of his mouth along with a look of gratitude.

"Sir, can you hear me?" Candace asked nervously. "What is your name, sir? Is your name Blalock, Warren Blalock?" she asked as he shook his head in the affirmative. "Do you know where you are?" Again he shook his head. "Do you feel as if you need a doctor?" and again his answer was yes.

"A doctor, hell he needs a hospital full of them it looks like to me," said Jack. "Mr. Blalock, we are going to get you some help so don't you worry, but first I need to know if you know a man name Ray Putnam. He has been missing for years just like you. I'm looking for him.

Again do you know this man?" Jack held up an old army photo of Ray. "Look at this picture. Do you know him?"

He drank a few more swallows of water hoping it would help him talk better. Then the name came out. "Rain Man," he said in a soft and low voice. "He liked to be called Rain Man." Jack stood straight, not believing what he had just heard. Harry patted Jack on the back. There were smiles all around the group.

"Mr. Blalock, where is he? Do you know where Ray, or Rain Man, is? Mr. Blalock, do you know his whereabouts sir?" The beaten prisoner looked up at Jack and grabbed his arm to help steady himself as he answered.

"He, he was tortured. We both were, for weeks. Soldiers were dealing drugs, selling to US officials." He stopped talking to take another drink of water then he started again.

"Rain Man, where is Ray Putnam, Mr. Blalock? Where's Ray?" Jack asked.

"We both . . . tortured for weeks. I escaped, he didn't make it. I'm so sorry," the man said with tears in his swollen eyes. "He didn't make it out. He saved my life. They killed him!"

Jack would not hear of it as he asked for the 10th time and kept pointing to Ray's picture. "No, this man, where is he? His name is Ray Putnam," Jack shouted, as he refused to accept the prisoner's answer.

The prisoner looked back at Jack for one last time. "Ray . . . his best friend. Steve. Hotel-Steve, right?" And with that the man closed his eyes and lay his head on the table. Jack knew right then the five-year search for Ray Putnam was over. And the US was using the government-backed soldiers to help ship drugs and money to Colombia. All was answered in those two words, Hotel Steve.

"He's gone, Jack," said Harry as he grabbed Jack and pulled him back. "I'm so sorry, my friend, but your man didn't make it, he's gone Jack!"

"Me too, Jack, I'm so sorry," the young lady said with tears in her eyes. Jack got up from his seat and walked away. He circled the room several times around until reality finally set in enough to allow Jack to accept the man's answer about Ray. He walked over and placed his hand on his shoulder as if to say thank you.

Lieutenant Perez returned along with the Chief of Police, Senior Juan Hernandez. As the two men entered the room Chief Hernandez acted as if he was appalled and demanded his men remove the chains from the prisoner, as he began to inspect the prisoner himself. In Spanish Chief Hernandez started shouting to his men.

"You don't have to know Spanish very well to understand a good old-fashioned ass whipping, now do you?" said Jack, as he looked over at Harry and Candace.

Within a few minutes an ambulance arrived at the police station. While EMTs attended to the prisoner, Lieutenant Perez gathered all the paperwork that was needed. The prisoner was loaded into an ambulance and soon they left to go to the nearest hospital. At least that was what the group was told.

Soon they too were out of the police station and headed back to the airport. Hardly a word was spoken on the return trip. Rhys and the other men greeted Jack as they awaited his return at customs in the airport terminal. Everyone that knew Ray took the news of his death hard. After all these years it still didn't lessen the blow. Jack had started thinking about what he was going to say in his letter to Ray's wife, Irene. It certainly would not be a shock, but the finality of it all would be painful nevertheless. Soon everyone was back in the Hawker Beechcraft.

Rhys and Jack sat in the cockpit ready to taxi down the runway as Rhys remembered Ray. "You know, Jack, that damn Ray, he sure was a good man. He really could drive the hell out of a Deuce and a Half truck."

"He sure could, Rhys, he certainly could."

Within minutes they were once again airborne as Jack headed the Hawker and its somber crew back home to Maryland, knowing they had lost another brother in arms.

What Can Brown Do for You?

Chapter 35

CONNIE WALKED INTO THE KITCHEN AND POURED herself a glass of water while noticing the small brown box still sitting on the counter that had been there for days. I wonder what's in the box; it must be something Jack ordered, she thought. As she again examined the package like she had numerous times before she set it back down on the counter and left the kitchen on her way to her office. Tricks the cat was stretched out asleep in the sunniest of windows while Jack was working in his study.

Connie worried about Jack; he hadn't been himself since his trip back from Venezuela. He wouldn't tell her much. She knew not to ask, she also knew he would get around to it and tell her about the whole situation but she knew now was not the time. He wasn't ready. She could tell he had been damaged by it, and getting over it would take love and time.

As for their Venezuelan FBI case, Matt Baranski said it was still ongoing, but like most open cases it was at a standstill and soon would become cold and forgotten. Getting a court order to investigate the CIA or FBI would be next to impossible to achieve. Besides, there was no public outcry and the government had a way of covering their tracks, for now anyway, Connie thought.

As for the Wessons, Bob and Nancy had left the country, but this time it was for that second honeymoon vacation Nancy had always wanted. No charges were ever filed and to Matt Baranski's dismay, out of the blue, the case was reclassified and placed into cold file status. But that wasn't good enough for Jack; he still had more questions and truly wondered how in the world Bob Wesson was ever able to hide his secret life from everyone, especially from Jack, after all these years. Something didn't add up. Nevertheless, Bob went back working and running his insurance company once again as if nothing had ever happened.

As for poor Tommy Riddle, he had been buried two weeks earlier and received a police funeral with full honors, which he deserved. What a sweet boy he was, Connie thought.

Connie was thinking to call Kay and see if she wanted to go shopping or maybe catch a movie. She was really hoping Kay's and Rhys's relationship would become one of being more than friends, but she knew better. Those two liked playing the field too much. Besides, being good friends is what it's all about anyway, she thought.

Her mind turned back to Jack who had been cooped up in that study of his for days now, working on a paper dealing with his thoughts about the whole South American drug cartel thing. He was hoping to present it to the US Congress or at least the Joint Chiefs of Staff. Ray Putnam, and the others that served with Jack and died for their country, deserved at least that much.

All these deep thoughts were running through her head as she stood in the living room. She heard the door to Jack's study open as he shouted to her.

"Hey Babe, what do you say we get the old convertible out and go for a Sunday afternoon drive just so we can get out of the house for a little bit? I'm tired of being cooped up in that little room. What do you say?" He moved towards Connie and grabbed her with his big arms and gave her a great big hug and a kiss on the cheek. He knew she could not refuse that kind of invitation as her legs danced in the air as he held her tight. Plus she hadn't seen Jack look that happy in a long time and she was not about to spoil the moment. The heck with the thoughts of shopping or going to see some old movie, Kay would just have to wait.

"Sure thing, sweetheart, give me a minute. Let me powder my nose, get my hat and sunglasses, and I'll be ready in a second," she said, as she kissed him again and headed off to the bathroom to freshen up.

Jack seemed to be in a real good mood as he walked around the kitchen counter looking for a quick snack. And there sitting on the counter was that brown box, the same package that had arrived by UPS several days earlier. Is nobody going to claim it? Jack thought. He once again inspected the small brown package all the while looking and shaking it as his curiosity was finally getting the best of him. He tried to figure out who sent it. Strangely there were no markings other than their address, no company logos. Not even a return address of any kind was on the small brown shoe-box size box. It must be something Connie ordered, probably from the Spiegel catalog, he thought. He was hoping for something better, maybe from Victoria's Secret. "Hey Babe, let's go," he called out.

"Hold on honey, I'll be out in one second." Staring in the mirror Connie applied a little more lipstick and swiftly gave her hair a quick brushing.

Without much thought Jack laid the plain brown box back down on top of the kitchen counter. Before grabbing an apple from a large bowl of fruit that was sitting on the kitchen table he reached over and grabbed the car keys off the key hook that was hanging on the wall beside the back door.

"Oh, what the heck," he said to himself as he turned back to the kitchen and retrieved the box off the counter top. He looked at the package and inspected it once again but this time he decided to open it. His fingers tore off some of the brown paper, but in the process he dropped it. He bent over and picked it up and shook it a couple of times, listening in hopes he didn't break the surprise gift. At the same time he talked loud enough so Connie could hear him.

"Hey Babe, who sent you this box, do you know?"

"Sorry dear, I can't hear you. Did you say box, the one you put on the kitchen counter about a week ago? What about it? I thought that was yours." She laid the hair brush down and fluffed her hair, staring into the mirror one last time before leaving the room. She turned the door knob to open the door.

Then it happened! In one swift moment the blast of blinding white light from the explosion flashed in Jack's face. Bystanders and other witness said they heard the explosion for miles as the blast completely incinerated Jack and most of the house. Instantly walls, windows, and doors were blown out and off their frame along with several rooms as the rest of the home was completely leveled. The fireball was seen for miles. Neighbors, in shock, ran out of their houses to witness the horrifying sight.

"Like being in a war zone," one neighbor said.

"I thought a plane crashed. The blast knocked me off my feet," another neighbor told the news crew who were broadcasting from the scene as the burning and broken house lay in ruins, and the fire burned on.

The explosion threw Connie hard against the bathroom wall, instantly knocking her unconscious as she fell into the bathtub, which probably saved her life. The bathroom ceiling gave way falling in and on top of her as she lay knocked out cold by the incredible blast. Connie never knew what happened. Soon fire crews arrived, digging and sifting through the debris and mayhem. Firemen fought and clawed their way through the wreckage, battling heavy black smoke and extreme heat and flames caused by broken gas lines.

"Hey man, over here, I think I found somebody," cried out one of the firemen as he stumbled into what was left of the bathroom. Several more men fought their way toward his voice in the back section of the home. Wrestling through the dust, debris, and smoke, the first fireman arrived and grabbed Connie by her shoulders while checking for a pulse. He then pulled her closer and placed an oxygen mask over her broken and bloody face.

The flames intensified while others manned the hoses and sprayed a safety blanket of water over both Connie and the firefighter. The fireman then pulled her up close to his body to lift her out of the tub. Suddenly a huge chunk of ceiling broke off, hitting Connie squarely in the back, causing both her and the fireman to fall on top of each other and land hard against the porcelain tub. More firemen came to the rescue pulling off debris as they used their axes to create an opening exit, which saved the whole team just in the nick of time. Suddenly the rest of the house collapsed into the yard, the onlookers jumping back to safety.

News of the explosion spread fast to friends and colleagues of Connie's and Jack's through the military and police community. Rhys got word and quickly contacted Kay. Both arrived at the house in minutes and watched as Connie was carried out of the house. There was no sign of Jack. Rhys stayed to help search for his best friend while Kay rode with Connie in the ambulance. It soon arrived at the John Hopkins Hospital, one of the finest in Baltimore.

Kay had called ahead to notify the staff of her friend's arrival. The doctors worked for hours removing shrapnel-like debris from Connie's fractured body. Both legs were broken along with her right arm, several broken ribs, and her collarbone. One large piece of metal was lodged directly beside her spinal cord in the small of her back. The doctors were hesitant to remove it, knowing there was a good chance she would never walk again, but they had no choice. It was the only way to save her life.

Kay and Rhys knew it would be several days in the hospital before Connie would know of her loss of Jack, and months of rehabilitation would be required due to the extent of her injuries. Kay and Rhys, along with other dear friends, surrounded Connie with the love and support she would need to heal. She would forever have the memories of her hero and husband, Jack Womack.

The Package Is Delivered

Chapter 36

Three weeks earlier . . .

THE SAME UPS TRUCK THAT HAD LEFT JACK'S AND CONNIE'S HOUSE a few miles back pulled up behind a parked black SUV that had been waiting along the street in this nondescript suburban neighborhood for quite some time. The driver of the truck was a large man with tanned skin and dark hair. He was careful to look up and down the street of the neighborhood making sure the coast was clear before he turned off the engine. He then stood up, having to duck his head as his large-framed body stepped back into the cargo section of the brown step van. He then shut the door behind him.

He knew that he had only a few seconds, not minutes, before the DIAD (Delivery Information Acquisition Device) system would locate the parked truck. The DIAD was the hand-held computer that each driver used to scan boxes for deliveries and pickups. It worked basically like a GPS and tracked every move the truck made. Soon the company would realize something was wrong, and only the driver knew the code to his or her DIAD.

The driver moved quickly as he removed a brown ball cap and replaced it with his own Boston Red Sox cap. He removed the company's iconic brown suit of both shorts and shirt and replaced it with a pair of his own jeans and a Re-elect Bill Clinton T-shirt, which covered his Army Ranger tattoo. He then placed the brown uniform into a black plastic trash bag and hastily started to clean up, grabbing a few boxes that had fallen from their shelves.

As he picked up the scattered boxes along the floor he saw the company driver's body lying among the fallen cargo. He removed the name tag, Andy, and tossed it on the deceased body. With trash bag in hand he removed his gloves. He stopped before he exited the vehicle and placed the gloves in the bag as well. He paused briefly as he looked in all directions, making sure the ordinary neighborhood still looked ordinary. He noticed children playing across the way, but they didn't notice him. He nonchalantly walked over to the parked SUV and motioned to the driver to pop open the trunk. Placing the trash bag inside, he proceeded to get into the passenger side of the vehicle.

"It took you long enough. Where were you? I was worried sick," asked the pretty blonde as he slid into the seat.

"It's all good girl, let's go," he ordered as she started the car.

"I waited long enough for you to get out of prison. You scared me, any problems?" she inquired before driving out of the neighborhood. The large black SUV was totally undetected by any bystanders.

"No worries my sweet Kimberly. We're together now for good, no problems at all. The package has been delivered," Cecil informed the young lady driving the car.

"Good, I wouldn't want my husband's death to have been in vain," she laughed, as she waited for the traffic light to turn green.

"I don't think you have anything to worry about, Mrs. Gambaro," as he reached over and the two kissed. The stoplight changed back to green and she drove a few more blocks till they heard and saw the sounds and sights of the busy interstate highway. She turned onto the southbound interstate and headed south out of DC. A few minutes down the road she slowly leaned over, afraid she might startle him. She softly touched his arm to get his attention.

"Cecil, sweetheart, sorry, but how long is this trip to Charleston going to take?"

"About eight and a half, maybe nine hours, sweetheart, depending on how many times you have to go to the bathroom," said the big man as he pulled the brim of his cap down over his eyes and laid the seat back. "About eight hours till I'm finally home," he whispered under his breath as he lay back in his seat to rest.

Cecil looked at his watch just before he closed his eyes. He knew it would be only minutes now before lack of movement from the UPS truck would attract attention, causing the terminal dispatcher to send another truck to investigate the situation once they arrived at the scene.

That notification would come in quickly, he thought, as the second UPS driver would arrive and find Andy's truck. And he couldn't forget the kids who were playing not too far from where he had parked the UPS van. They probably noticed the truck, which seemed to have been parked there for quite some time. He wondered how long it would be before curiosity got the best of them and they questioned why the van was still there, and one of the kids opened the cargo door. It would be something they would never forget, that's for sure, Cecil thought.

The driver of the second truck pulled in behind the van. He looked down at the kids as he turned off the engine and stepped out. Still shaking from what they had seen, the kids weren't about to say a word to the new driver. They silently watched him step into the van. There on the floor under a few boxes he saw the lifeless body of poor Andy. Suddenly in his haste he fell backward as he quickly tried to get out of the truck as soon as possible. He eventually got to his feet again and quickly ran back to his truck calling the terminal's dispatcher, who immediately called 911.

Yeah, that's the way it will happen, Cecil imagined, as a smile appeared on his face. His plan was years in the making. He had it all planned out in his mind just how it would go down, even how the police would arrive, and how four kids were still standing beside the truck with blank stares on their little faces as the shock of what they had just seen was finally sinking in.

Cecil was feeling pretty good at this point, with no worries as the car he was riding in was taking him closer to home with every mile as they headed south out of town on interstate 95. A smile once again appeared on his face.

But soon the smile on his face vanished, knowing he had unfinished business once he arrived back home. He had the Gambaro insurance money tucked away. That was no problem, but what to do with her, Kimberly Gambaro? The cops would soon be looking for her for questioning after the Womacks' deaths, if not already. Besides she was no longer of any use. Sure she was a good lay, but there would be many more like her, he thought.

Soon, in about 460 miles, she would become another missing person. That was about the distance till they would reach Lake Marion. That night they would check-into a hotel room in the small town of Santee, which was on that lake. They would probably have dinner at Clark's, one of Cecil's favorite places to eat back in the day, as hunger pains started to creep in. The smile reappeared on his face as he closed his eyes and lay back in the leather seats of the SUV feeling reassured. He patted Kimberly on the leg as she drove, and she smiled too. Yeah things were going to work out just fine, he thought, after all, they had so far.

But what Cecil didn't know was that homicide detective Tommy Riddle, acting alone without his partner Matt, would soon arrive at the scene and take complete charge of the investigation. He made sure the area was completely secured and roped off for the forensic team as they started taking photographs, dusting for prints in and outside of the van, and searching other vehicles along the roadside. They set up police lines throughout the quarantined area that covered several blocks of the neighborhood in their search for clues. Tommy made sure no one touched anything while the body was sent to the morgue for an autopsy in hopes of more clues.

Unfortunately, all of that stopped after Tommy's death. The forensic reports were never completed, along with the autopsy report that was never filed. And just like that another cold case was born. And as to

Kimberly Gambaro, ironically shortly after her interview at police headquarters with her new lawyer, Kim Gambaro was never heard from or seen again. Her body was never found, and she was still listed as a missing person.

Web
We Weave

Chapter 37

BOB WESSON HURRIEDLY UNLOCKED HIS OFFICE DOOR. He moved as if time was of the essence. Keeping his entry a secret, he didn't dare turn on the overhead lights. He quickly proceeded across the dark room to his large oak desk where he sat down behind it and turned on a small desk lamp. He opened the top desk drawer and removed the file cabinet key. He turned his chair to face the oak cabinets and quickly unlocked and pulled several file drawers open from a beautiful wall of wooden file cabinets behind his desk. He grabbed the desk lamp and turned the shade in his direction.

One by one Bob opened each file and checked its contents. He either removed the information or placed it back into the file folder and went to the next file jacket. This scenario played out for a few more minutes till every file folder had been reviewed and removed from the cabinet to his briefcase or placed back into its familiar home in the wall of beautiful hardwoods. No need to turn on any computer for this, he thought, as he started to look back over at his collection of his best-of-the-best clients.

In his mind he started to count the accumulation of wealth from each portfolio. With all the information he had in those files, from social security numbers, birthdays, mothers' maiden names, addresses, offshore bank accounts, signatures, etc., he had more than enough information to transfer their insurance equity to his own bank accounts in the Cayman Islands.

Then Bob suddenly heard a noise. He was startled as he heard a man's cough, someone clearing his throat in the corner of the large dark office. He had no idea someone had been there the whole time as he quickly looked up. The look of shock was immediate on his face as he was not only surprised by the intrusion, but he also recognized the voice of the man sitting in the shadows of the corner as he spoke.

"Well, Monsieur Wesson, my, my, aren't you the clever one. But you seem to be in a great deal of hurry this evening. Is everything OK?"

Bob didn't ask the man how he got into his office. There was no need. Bob just waited in silence for a few seconds. The mere sight of this small man with the French accent wearing a bright yellow suit under a trench coat troubled Bob to his core. Goose bumps covered his skin. The hairs on the back of his neck stood at attention. The sheer sight of this man would strike fear in all who found themselves on his wrong side. Plus there was the fear of the person the small man worked for. And Bob knew all too well of this man's tremendous power and motivation. Bob's dry mouth managed to speak a few words as the two stared at each other.

"It's been a long time, Monsieur. Let's see, I believe I have not seen you in what, 15 maybe 20 years," Bob answered. Suddenly the little man stood up and walked closer to the large oak desk Bob was seated behind. He then stopped abruptly and turned to look out the large picture window and began to stomp his foot on the floor repeatedly, and then stopped. He turned back and saw Bob, who was physically shaking at this point.

"It's been over 20 years, Robert. I believe Daniel's body lay about right here, didn't it?" questioned the little man.

"Yes, I believe it did, yes sir," Bob nervously answered, as the little man walked closer.

"Why didn't you call me, Robert? That's all you had to do and this mess would have never happened." He walked closer and leaned on the large desk staring directly into Bob's eyes.

"Well, well I, I tried!" Beads of sweat now appeared on Bob's face. He pulled at his tie to loosen the strain. "Look, Monsieur, I'm sorry but I—" The man suddenly slapped his hand on the desk as Bob jumped in his seat.

"No, you had to call her, didn't you? Why Robert, why her of all people? You know she is the one person who would find our mistakes. And she did, didn't she? And of course she would reveal them to the authorities."

"I'm sorry, I had no idea she would find out anything. Hell, I don't know if she really did after all of this," he cried.

"Oh no, she found out enough, Robert. She found plenty, and look at the cost."

"Now you just wait a minute. I did my job deflecting the focus off the organization and if you can't see that then the hell with all of you."

"Deflect the focus, you know nothing you stupid man. You deflected nothing. You just got more people involved. That's all you did, Robert, and that got people killed."

"Who, people like Danny and Sam? No one told me those two were expendable and why, because they knew the truth about you and the organization. Again, I was trying to deflect the investigation from the organization, not to it."

"Everyone is expendable Robert, including you and me."

"Well, fine, but I'm telling you the police don't know shit, besides I've got a man there too. Trust me, you still need me and you know it!"

"Do you have any idea what you have done, or the trouble you have caused the organization?"

"Look, the man died right here in my office. What else was I to do?"

"Think of all those people that had to be hurt because of your ignorance, Robert."

Bob sat up straight in his chair placing both hands on his desk and with his newfound courage he shouted, "Then damn you, if you are not going to listen to reason then screw you and the organization. I've been a good soldier for you people, for years, and you know it! And if that doesn't count for anything, well, the hell with it and the hell with you too."

That was it. Bob had had enough. There was nothing else to say as he waited for his sentencing or punishment. Feeling confident and at peace he eased back in his chair, closed his eyes, and waited. A few seconds went by and nothing happened. He slowly opened his eyes one at a time.

"OK, Robert, I hear you. I agree you could still be important to us, but again you brought this on yourself and you know it. And by the way you can put those files back. You're not going anywhere." He then paused and turned back as he walked back across the office floor to the door and stopped where Danny once lay. The little man looked back slightly over his shoulder without looking directly at Bob. "Be extremely careful, Robert. We would not wish any harm to happen to you and of course that nice wife of yours, now would we?" Bob watched as the man turned his head back around and slowly strolled out of the dark office. He shut the door behind him.

With a sinking sensation of feeling numb, Bob stared at the closed door. The minutes ticked by. A tsunami of reality came crashing in with the realization that he had just placed himself on the wrong side of the wrong man. He looked down at his briefcase full of files knowing now that was not a choice; no money in the world could help him now. He reflected back on his double life. It was one of a successful business man and the other of a spy, and both were nothing but lies in which he betrayed his employees, loved ones, and friends. He pushed his chair back from the desk. With no real exit plan to think of, he felt compelled to pull open the bottom right-hand desk drawer. He hesitated briefly while he stared at the nickel-plated revolver, a Smith and Wesson snub-nosed .38 caliber. His hands started to shake. He studied his options.

The End

From the author:

As always, I would like to take this time to thank each and every one of my readers for choosing to read my books. It is such a treat and an honor; I truly hope that you did enjoy the journey once again with Connie, Jack, Rhys, and the whole gang. Connie Womack will soon be back solving more crimes of murder and intrigue in the next book in her series.

Don't forget to please take time and go to **Amazonbooks.com** and write a review. If you can't write a good review, please wait for my next book! No, seriously, please write one. A good review is very helpful to an author and helps my books get noticed faster. Thank you in advance for your time. Once again, I thank you all, and please tell a friend on Facebook or other social media. It will be greatly appreciated.

Sincerely,

Wm. Brent Hensley

To the Boo Crew;

This book would not have been possible without the hard work of my editing team starting with my favorite member, who happens to be the love of my life, my wife Kay. Her input turns my scribble into complete sentences. Every day with her has been a blessing and a tremendous honor. How lucky I am to know her, much less be able to love her each day.

Next I would like to thank my dear friend, Phil Owens with DOCS Publishing. He is a true wordsmith and somehow manages to correct all the little mistakes I miss, and trust me that is a lot. Phil is a true professional.

The rest of the Boo Crew consists of more dear friends who proofread my work, making sure my words flow and helping catch any punctuation or grammar that needs to be corrected. Their most valuable contribution however is just being a great sounding board during the writing process.

I truly want to thank all of you for your hard work and honest input, but mostly for your love and support. It's a team effort in this writing business and you need all the love and support you can get.

Thank you as always,

Brent

Made in the USA
Columbia, SC
21 May 2022

60726963R00183